Madison sat up in her chair. This guy sounded interesting. He was funny, yet serious. A major bonus: He liked Cherry Garcia, which was her second-favorite flavor of ice cream. Madison knew she should be paying attention to Ms. Healy's lecture, but she wanted to respond immediately. Since Madison had already chewed the tops off all her fingernails, she nibbled on a pencil as she tried to decide what to say to this guy. She remembered Mr. Wheeler's words: "Be honest and go with the flow!"

P9-CPY-123

PERFECT STRANGERS

Jahnna N. Malcolm

♥ Simon Pulse ♥

New York   London   Toronto   Sydney

This story is for you, Skye.
It would not have happened without you.

SIMON PULSE
An imprint of Simon & Schuster
Children's Publishing Division
1230 Avenue of the Americas
New York, NY 10020
Copyright © 2005 by
Jahnna Beecham and Malcolm Hillgartner
All rights reserved, including the right of
reproduction in whole or in part in any form.
SIMON PULSE and colophon are registered trademarks
of Simon & Schuster, Inc.
Designed by Ann Zeak
Printed in United States of America
First Simon Pulse edition January 2005
2 4 6 8 10 9 7 5 3 1
Library of Congress Control Number 2004101685
ISBN 0-689-87221-6

1

Dear Heart-2-Heart pal,
Roses are red. Violets are blue. I am
a junior. How about you?
                    Your friend,
                    Guess who?

Madison McKay stared at her computer
screen and chewed on the last unbitten fingernail on her hand. It was a terrible letter,
no doubt about it. But her teacher, Mr.
Wheeler, had said, "Reveal something about
yourself and ask your pen pal a question."
Madison had covered all the bases, hadn't
she? Okay, so maybe she'd taken a few
shortcuts, but she couldn't help it. She was
having trouble concentrating.

"Ow!" Madison yelped, as she ripped her cuticle.

Mr. Wheeler looked up from his desk at the front of the room. "Madison? Are you having trouble with your computer?"

"It's not my computer," Madison replied, grinning sheepishly. "It's my brain. I think I left it at home."

Mr. Wheeler scooted back his chair. "Do you need help getting started?"

"Oh, no, no, no!" Madison called, horrified that her teacher might have to help her write a simple letter. "I was having trouble choosing the perfect words to describe my feelings, but I think I've got them now."

To prove that she was fine she placed her hands on her keyboard and wildly typed: *#xtyp nm4dg plafrhk vywkl asdayhxc sincerely xxxxxooopps yours yours yours.*

Usually a simple assignment like writing a letter to a pen pal would be a cinch for Madison. But she'd stayed up all night, tossing and turning, too excited to sleep. Today was the day Evergreen High School would nominate the candidates for student president and she was going to be one of them.

Madison had been planning for this day for nearly three years. Now that it was here, she was too nervous to concentrate on anything. Her brain was filled with cotton candy.

"Yo, Mr. Wheeler! When do we get to meet our Heart-2-Heart pals?" Robbie Leonis called from the back of the class.

"You're not supposed to meet them, Robbie. You're only supposed to write them. Didn't I make that clear?" Mr. Wheeler ran a hand over the dome of his bald head as he explained for the tenth time. "You, and all of the students at Evergreen, are to share your feelings and concerns with someone your own age. But you never have to worry that they'll tell anyone about you, because they won't know who you are. And vice versa."

"Too bad." Robbie tipped back his chair and set one black leather boot on the desk across from him. "I wrote a pretty cool letter."

Madison nearly choked. Robbie Leonis, the kid most likely to never turn in his homework, had already finished his assignment and she hadn't even started hers.

Emily Greenblatt raised her hand. "If we're not going to meet our Heart-2-Heart pals, how long do we have to write them?"

"We would like you to correspond for a month." Mr. Wheeler went over to the chalkboard, wrote *May 30* on it, and circled it. "After that, it's up to you whether or not you want to continue writing, or actually meet."

The Heart-2-Heart pen pal program was one of those big ideas that the Evergreen High counselors had invented to help students survive their high school years. Each student was given an anonymous e-mail address and assigned a Heart-2-Heart partner. As part of their twice-weekly advisor group meetings, students were supposed to communicate with their partners. The counselors hoped that students would be able to share their problems with each other, no matter how big or small.

Mr. Wheeler stood up and gave a general announcement to the students in the room. "Remember! Heart-2-Heart is about true feelings. Be honest and just go with the flow."

"You asked for it," Madison murmured as she deleted what was already on her screen. She took a deep breath and wrote the first thing that came into her head.

Dear Whatever-Your-Name-Is,

I resent being forced to write to a perfect stranger and share my innermost thoughts, but this is being graded. Also, everyone in class expects me to write this letter with a big perky smile because that's what I always do. Part of me would just like to skip school, catch a movie, eat cookie dough ice cream, dye my hair pink—or, better yet, shave my head—and party all night. But I'm trapped in an overachiever's body. You see, I'm working on maintaining a perfect GPA. How uptight is that? THERE! I've shared my innermost thoughts. Satisfied?

Pinky

Madison clicked SEND, stuffed her books into her pink nylon backpack, draped her purse over her shoulder, and waited for the bell to ring. She had to admit, once she'd actually *started* the assignment, it felt pretty good. Liberating, even. It was fun not having to impress anyone. Her parents and teachers always expected her to make straight A's. Other students automatically assumed Madison would be first in everything: first with the answer, first to turn in her homework, first to finish the exam.

What made it doubly hard was that everyone, including her best friends, thought Madison's success came easy. Only Madison knew how hard she had to work for her grades. She often stayed up past midnight to finish homework. She got up early to study and if she was confused, she stayed after school to ask for help. In short, she was a model student, and it was a bummer!

Madison leaned her chin on her hand and wondered about the lucky party who had just received her not-so-charming e-mail introduction. She was already starting to regret her impulsiveness. Maybe she shouldn't have been *quite* so straightforward about her feelings about Heart-2-Heart, and should not have gone off on all her troubles. What if the person she wrote to had real problems, and needed *her*?

"Earth to Madison!" a voice called from the fringes of her consciousness. "Wake uh-up!"

Madison blinked several times in confusion. She looked up to see a smiling face framed by short, dark pigtails and oversized wing tip glasses staring down at her. It was her best friend, Piper Chang. "I *am* awake,"

Madison replied. Then she noticed the empty classroom. "What happened to the rest of the class?"

"*They*"—Piper gestured to the rows of empty desks—"all thought the bell meant, 'Go to your next class.' Apparently you don't interpret it that way."

"Next class!" Madison bolted out of her seat in alarm. "I'm going to be late."

"Correction. You *are* late." Piper pointed to the round clock above the door. "Two minutes late, to be exact. However, in your case, it doesn't matter."

"Are you crazy? I've got calculus with Hooper this period," Madison said, scooping her books into her arms. "Tardiness always matters with Hooper."

"Excuse me." Piper folded her arms across her chest and tapped her foot impatiently. "Aren't we forgetting something?"

Madison patted her shoulder for her purse, checked her books in her backpack, and made sure her PalmPilot was in the zipper pocket. "No, I don't think so, Piper. Give me a clue."

"The assembly next period? Hello?" Piper slid her bright purple glasses down to the tip of her nose. "Alex Kazinsky is nominating you for school president, and I am seconding the nomination."

"Oh, the election!" Madison slapped her forehead with her palm. "How could I forget?"

After tossing and turning half the night, Madison had pulled herself out of bed an hour earlier than her usual six A.M. to make sure she'd have time to get ready. It had taken a half hour to get her short dark hair to wisp in just the right places so that it framed her face and emphasized her big brown eyes. She'd tried on three different outfits before finally settling on a pink cashmere sweater with a rolled collar, a pink-and-brown-plaid kilt skirt, and white over-the-knees stockings that she hoped gave her the earnest but highly fashionable schoolgirl look she was aiming for.

"I think this Heart-2-Heart assignment really got me rattled," Madison confessed. "I mean, what can you say to someone you don't know? I just didn't know how to get started."

"I thought it was a piece of cake," Piper said as she linked arms with Madison and pulled her toward the classroom door. "I merely described myself, gave my initials, P. C., reminded my pen pal that the nominating assembly was next period, and warned him or her that they'd better vote for Madison McKay—or else!"

Madison shook her head. "Piper, you told them everything. They'll figure out who you are."

Piper stopped to raise a purple lacquered nail. "Ah, but I left out a few very telling details. Like the fact that my mother is Swedish but my dad is Chinese. And nowhere in the entire correspondence did I even mention my perfect 4.0, or that I was the very first student at Evergreen High to own a MINI Cooper."

"But what about your innermost thoughts?" Madison asked. "Didn't you share any of those?"

"I don't have innermost thoughts," Piper said brightly. "They look just like my outermost thoughts."

Madison chuckled. That was true. Whatever went into Piper's head came out of her mouth, which made her a little too blunt for comfort sometimes. But Madison liked that her friend was bold—in words and in dress.

Today Piper was sporting typical Piper apparel: purple-and-lime green polka-dot mini, purple vest, and lemon yellow tee with her trademark candy apple red high tops—all from her favorite place—Urban Outfitters. Her motto was, "No color is too bright or skirt too tight!" Madison wished she could be more like her.

"Piper, you are truly out there," Madison said, draping an arm around her best friend's shoulder.

"That's right." Piper took a stick of gum from her heart-shaped purse and folded it in half. "With me, what you see is what you get." She pushed open the door into the hall. "Now, come on."

Madison took one step out the door and froze. The hall was totally deserted except for the one person Madison did not want to see: Jeremy Drum. He stood at his open locker, dropping books into a gray-and-black backpack. Just the sight of him made Madison's stomach do flip-flops.

"What's the holdup?" Piper called, giving Madison a shove from behind.

"Could you just wait a second?" Madison hissed. "*He's* out there."

Piper didn't have to ask who *he* was. She already knew. Jeremy Drum—Madison's nemesis. At Homecoming their freshman year he had managed to totally humiliate Madison in front of a stadium full of people. The prank easily rated a perfect "10" for meanness, which hadn't won Jeremy any friends with the students or teachers. It certainly had made a permanent enemy of Madison.

Madison waited for Jeremy to close his locker and move on. He slipped a black sport coat over his gray T-shirt and jeans, and shut the metal door with a loud *clang*. He jerked back when he spotted her in the doorway.

"Whoa," he murmured, shaking his jet-black hair away from his forehead. His pale blue eyes looked at her evenly. "I didn't see you there."

Madison was too flustered to speak. Instead, she turned and marched straight into the girls' bathroom at the other end of the corridor. Her cheeks were blazing hot.

Piper was right behind her. "Way to handle Jeremy. Just run!"

"I don't know why he still gets to me,

but I just can't forget what happened," Madison said, flicking on the faucet in the sink and splashing cold water on her face. "I look at him and I remember Homecoming, and practically break out in hives." She yanked a paper towel out of the dispenser and blotted her face dry. "It's stupid. I know."

"Nobody expects you to forget." Piper pulled a lime green makeup bag from her purse. She patted the shine off her own nose, then turned and powdered Madison's nose. "But everyone else has. We're almost to the end of our junior year, Mad. Time to move on."

"You're right." Madison fluffed her hair back into place. Then she applied a slight frosting of MAC to her lips. "That was then, this is now."

"That's the spirit." Piper sprayed a short burst of Gap Heaven perfume on her own neck, and then on Madison's. Next she tightened each of the short pigtails above her ears. The effect made her look like an Asian Pippi Longstocking.

"There are over a thousand students in this school," Madison continued, "and he's just one guy."

"An extremely hunky kind of guy," her friend interjected.

"Piper!" Madison dug her elbow into Piper's side.

"But he's a snake, and we'll just forget he ever existed," Piper finished quickly.

"Right." Madison checked her reflection in the mirror one more time as the bell rang. The assembly was about to begin. "So let's rock."

The two friends stepped into the Main Hall of Evergreen High, ready to take on the world.

2

The noise in Evergreen's auditorium was deafening as twelve hundred students scrambled to find seats for the big assembly. The auditorium, like the rest of Evergreen High, had been built in the 1920s, and was a beautiful art deco structure with dark wood paneling. The seats in the front center rows were covered in heavy red velvet, and it was a given that they were for seniors only. Freshmen didn't even dare venture down there. Sophomores and juniors filled up the middle and sides on the main floor. The ninth graders took the back of the hall. There was also a balcony, but that was rarely filled except for an all-school event like this one. The kids who sat up there were the fringe groups—"Skaters, loners, and stoners," as Piper called them.

"Maddy! Maddy McKay!" someone called from down by the stage. Madison didn't even have to look to know who it was. It was her pal Alex Kazinsky, Drama Club president and all-around school cutup. He was the only one who called her Maddy. She could see Alex's flaming red hair bouncing up and down over the heads of several boys from the basketball team. Alex was taller than any of them, but he was no jock. He looked more like the Scarecrow in *The Wizard of Oz,* all elbows and angles. Which was why he had been cast in that part when Evergreen put on *The Wiz* during their freshman year. His loose-limbed dancing style and beautiful tenor voice made him a shoo-in for all the musicals.

Madison tried to weave her way through the mob of students. Every few seconds someone would pat her on the back and say, "Good luck, Madison. You've got my vote." She wanted to stop and chat with each supporter, but she couldn't because Piper was pushing her down the aisle.

"Quit shoving so hard," Madison protested. "I'm going to fall down or run over somebody."

That only made Piper push harder. "Alex saved us a seat down front, but we're going to lose it if we don't get there soon. You know the cheerleading squad. They insist on being in the front row."

They came to an abrupt halt as a blond cheerleader riding piggyback on a friend blocked their way. The cheerleader waved her arms wildly and yelled, "Madison, we're behind you all the way!"

"Thanks, Samantha," Madison shouted over the din. "That's awesome."

Suddenly a long arm snaked out from behind Samantha and pulled Madison between a couple who were sharing an extra-slobbery kiss.

Madison found herself face-to-face—or face-to-chest—with Alex Kazinsky.

"Alex! Why do I have to come all the way down to the front?" Madison shrieked over the noise of the other students. "It's like a mosh pit down here!"

Alex gestured upward with his thumb. "I'm running a secret light check."

High above them a tiny person with short brown hair and a dark hooded sweatshirt waved from her position in the light grid.

"Mouse will hit you with a follow spot when I announce your nomination," Alex explained. "She needs to know exactly where you're going to be when you stand up. We need a dress rehearsal."

Madison saw that Alex had reserved a front-row seat for her in the center section. He was definitely treating this nominating assembly as if it were a performance. She took two steps away from the seat and waved up to Mouse. "How's this?"

Mouse got her in her sights and focused the spot, turning the intensity of the light up just a little.

"Don't look up," Alex warned Madison. "I didn't clear the spotlight with Mrs. Van Reenan. She'll be miffed, but only for a minute or two."

Standing on tiptoe, Madison wrapped her arms around her friend's neck and gave him a tight squeeze. "Thank you, Alex. You are so amazing."

"I know," Alex said with a grin. "That's why all the girls love me."

Piper tugged on Madison's jacket. "Al is walking to the mike. We need to sit down."

"Al" was Piper's code word for the principal, Mr. Kaufman. She called him Al because, with his big bushy mustache and wild cloud of gray hair, he looked like Albert Einstein.

As Mr. Kaufman adjusted the microphone, Madison settled into her seat and tried to stay calm. Why did she feel so nervous? This was what she had been dreaming about since middle school. She had her two best friends on either side of her, ready to stand by her every step of the way.

Madison took a couple of deep breaths to calm the feeling of panic creeping up her spine. In just a few minutes the nominations would take place, and her life would kick into overdrive. She already felt overwhelmed with her load of AP classes, after-school clubs, and work on the yearbook and newspaper. Adding a run for student body president seemed insane.

Mr. Kaufman blew into the microphone a few times to make sure it was working. "Hello? Hello? Can you hear me out there?"

The obligatory "No!" came singing out of the balcony. The principal ignored the scattered laughter and waited for the students to settle down.

"Good morning, everyone. Welcome to Evergreen High's seventy-fifth nominating assembly," Mr. Kaufman's voice boomed over the PA. "This is a pivotal moment in every school year. Today you nominate the students who will lead you through the next school year. None of us here at Evergreen take this lightly, because our high school leaders today will be the leaders of our country tomorrow."

The principal's words provoked a groan that rippled down from the balcony into the students sitting below. Even Piper, who could easily win a Most School Spirit award, leaned toward Madison and murmured, "Cornball."

The principal went on to explain the nominating process. "You cannot nominate yourself. Two students are needed for each nomination—one to make the nomination, and another to second it."

Mr. Kaufman described in detail the

responsibilities of each elected officer, from class representative to president. He emphasized that the president not only ran all student council meetings but represented the student body to the community at large.

"Remember, your president is your liaison with the world outside these walls," the principal concluded. "Choose wisely."

Mr. Kaufman signaled the Evergreen Eagles pep band to play the school song and Madison felt a tingling surge of excitement—the one she always got when she was faced with a challenge. She glanced at Alex and Piper, who were clapping enthusiastically along with the rousing music, and realized how much she valued her friends and their unflagging support. She wasn't going to let them down!

"The floor is now open for nominations."

Alex bounded out of his seat and reached the microphone at the foot of the stage in one giant step. "Mr. Kaufman. Fellow students. The president of Evergreen High School needs to be more than just a brilliant student and organized leader. She needs to have vision, drive, and that extra spark that we in the theater call 'star quality.'

Madison McKay has that spark. She also has my nomination for president of Evergreen High."

The cheerleaders heard the cheering and automatically leaped to their feet, pumping their fists in the air.

Mr. Kaufman held up his hands for quiet and asked, "Is there a second?"

Piper was already at the microphone. "Hi, I'm Piper Chang, and I am proud to second the nomination of my friend, our next student body president—Madison McKay!"

The auditorium rocked with cheers and applause. Alex nudged Madison. "Okay, Maddy. It's showtime."

As Madison stood up, Mouse hit her with the spotlight and the crowd responded with even louder cheers. Her heart was pounding in her chest as she stepped up to the microphone. "Thank you, Alex. Thank you, Piper. And thank *you,* Evergreen High School. You are an amazing student body. I accept this nomination, and can't wait to see what kind of miracles will happen when we all put our heads together next year!"

Instantly Alex and Piper were at her side, raising her hands above her head like a boxing champion in the ring. It was a glorious moment, and as Madison basked in the glow of the applause, she wondered if anything could ever top it.

The next nomination was for Reed Rawlings, which came as no surprise. He'd been dropping hints all spring about wanting to run for president. The week before, he'd arrived at school with a bumper sticker on his BMW convertible that read, REED WILL LEAD. Dan Bladek, who quarterbacked the football team, made the nomination, which was seconded by the team's enormous center, Barton Lewis.

Reed entered from the back of the auditorium and came down the aisle, waving to the crowd like a seasoned politician. Maddy turned in her seat to watch her rival's entrance. Reed was tall and muscular, and moved with the fluid grace of a natural athlete. As all-city wide receiver for the Evergreen Eagles, Reed was one of the most recognized kids at school. His father was a wealthy heart surgeon, and a board member of the exclusive Rainier Club in downtown Seattle. No doubt Reed planned to follow in his father's footsteps.

Reed stepped up to the microphone and declared, "I accept this nomination from my fellow Screamin' Eagles."

Dan and the rest of the football team began to chant in unison, "Reed! Reed! Reed!"

Reed grinned, then motioned for them to stop. "I like a good challenge," he continued, "and look forward to an exciting race with my good friend Madison. May the best"—Reed winked slyly at Madison—"*man* win."

Piper and Alex groaned at the joke, but Madison laughed it off. Reed seemed so full of himself that it was hard to believe he could be a real threat.

After soaking in the applause for what seemed like a *long* time, Reed made his exit up the opposite aisle. He high-fived anyone who stuck out their hand as he went by.

Finally Mr. Kaufman approached the microphone again. He looked out at the auditorium and arched an eyebrow. "If there are no more nominations—"

"There's one more," a voice called from offstage. Mr. Kaufman squinted into the darkness, then flinched when a tall boy in faded jeans, a gray T-shirt, and a black sport jacket sauntered onto the stage.

"Jeremy Drum!" Piper and Alex gasped at the same moment. "No way!"

"You're supposed to speak into *that* microphone." Mr. Kaufman pointed at the other mike at the front of the stage.

Jeremy shrugged. "What's the difference? I'm here. Why don't I just make the nomination with yours?"

Mr. Kaufman sputtered for a few seconds but gave up and sat down.

Jeremy leaned too close to the microphone, and it screeched loudly. He jerked back his head and tried again. "Um, hello. I'm Jeremy Drum. I'm a pretty regular guy, like most of you out there. I'd like to nominate myself."

"You can't do that!" Mr. Kaufman cried, leaping to his feet. "Someone else has to do the nominating. Weren't you listening when I read the rules?"

The principal's words didn't seem to faze Jeremy. He shrugged and said, "All right. Nick Torres—you out there?"

"Dude. I'm here," a voice shouted down from the balcony.

Jeremy shielded his eyes against the stage lights and looked up in the direction of Nick's voice. "So who do you nominate for president?"

"You, man. Rock on."

The nomination was greeted with just a smattering of scattered applause.

Mr. Kaufman stood up once more. "You'll need a second, Mr. Drum."

Jeremy looked out to the back of the auditorium. "Any seconds?"

There was a moment of awkward silence.

"Yes," came a female voice from the back row. Sierra Faith stood up. She was Evergreen's resident flower child and was wearing her usual dreads, patchwork jeans, and hippie blouse. "I second Jeremy's nomination," she said in a reedy voice.

Jeremy looked back at Mr. Kaufman, who simply nodded. Jeremy shoved his hands into the pockets of his jeans and leaned forward into the mike. "I'm thrilled to accept the nomination from the back of the balcony and the back of the auditorium, which are just physical locations. No one at Evergreen High should take a backseat to anyone else. We're all equals on this

amazing bus ride, and none of you"—
Jeremy pointed to the balcony and sides of
the auditorium—"should forget it."

Jeremy looked calmly up at the balcony
and raised his fist. This time, the applause
was loud and enthusiastic. One of the
cheerleaders, a girl named Krystal Nivens,
jumped up to do a stag leap in support, until
the head cheerleader, Margot Peterson,
yanked her back down in her seat.

Alex and Piper didn't say anything. As
the audience cheered, they exchanged mean-
ingful looks. Madison knew exactly what
those looks meant: This election wasn't
exactly in the bag. Jeremy Drum had clearly
struck a responsive chord with many students. A half an hour ago it would have
sounded laughable, but now Madison had to
look at him as a serious contender.

Mr. Kaufman quickly brought the
assembly to a close. The principal tried to
dismiss the assembly one class at a time, but
no one paid any attention. Students climbed
over seats, leapfrogged up the aisles, and ran
out of the auditorium through the "emergency only" exit doors.

"Come on, Madison," Piper said. "Let's get out of here—if we can."

Madison saw what Piper meant. The aisles were still clogged with students, all talking about the surprise candidate. It was almost as hard to leave as it had been to come in.

"What happened to Alex?" Madison asked. "Wasn't he with us?"

Piper gestured with her thumb. "Over there."

Alex had been pulled toward the exit by the crowd. He'd hopped up onto the armrests of one of the seats and was waving at Madison until he caught her eye. When she waved to him, he mimed eating an extra-cheesy piece of pizza, pointed a finger to his temple, and wiggled his fingers like rain coming down.

"What's he saying?" Piper asked.

"I think he wants us to eat pizza and brainstorm," Madison translated.

Piper cupped her hands around her mouth and shouted to Alex, "When?

Alex put one hand to his chest and belted out the first few notes to the song "Tomorrow" from the musical *Annie.* He would have continued, but Coach Craig yanked him off the auditorium seat and he disappeared into the crowd.

Piper and Madison were still laughing when they got to the hall outside the auditorium. As the bell rang, Madison gave her best friend a quick hug. "That was a blast. Let's meet at Giorgio's tomorrow night at seven and let the fun continue."

"I'll tell the gang," Piper said as she jogged off in the opposite direction. "Later, gator!"

3

The whole assembly had been a major adrenaline rush for Madison, which made the rest of the day feel like she was wading through molasses.

Madison's last period was American Literature with Lorraine Healy, the Iron Maiden. Ms. Healy was the toughest grader at Evergreen High. A B from her was a triumph. An A was an absolute miracle.

The class was studying Hawthorne's classic American novel *The Scarlet Letter* and Ms. Healy was lecturing at length about it. Madison knew she ought to be taking detailed notes, but today she was finding it hard to focus. Just for a lark, Madison slipped her PalmPilot out of her purse.

Keeping it out of sight behind her desk, she logged on to her e-mail to see if her Heart-2-Heart pal had replied. Yes!

Dear Pinky,

Cookie Dough ice cream is great, but Cherry Garcia reigns supreme. I did the hair dye thing already, only I went blue. I looked like a Smurf. The good news is, I did it when I was visiting my cousins. The bad news is, the hair dye stained their sheets, and I had to buy them a new set. Inner thoughts: On the outside I'm the class clown, always ready with a wisecrack. On the inside, I'm a pretty serious guy. My secret wish: to start over.

Just call me Blue

Madison sat up in her chair. This guy sounded interesting. He was funny, yet serious. A major bonus: He liked Cherry Garcia, which was her second-favorite flavor of ice cream. Madison knew she should be paying attention to Ms. Healy's lecture, but she wanted to respond immediately. Since Madison had already chewed the tops off all her fingernails, she nibbled on a pencil as she tried to decide what to say to this guy. She remembered Mr. Wheeler's words: "Be honest and go with the flow!"

> Dear Blue,
> Do you think it's really possible to start over? I mean, without moving away to a new town? I think that even if I tried to change, my friends, family, and even my teachers wouldn't let me. No matter what I did, they'd go on assuming I'm this follow-the-rules, never-let-anybody-down kind of girl. So I guess I'll have to stick with their vision of me. However, once I graduate next year—I'm going to go wild! Pierce some body part and get a tattoo. Whoo-hoo! How about you? Ever been tat-tooed?
>
> Pinky

Madison sent her letter and slipped the PalmPilot back into her purse. Everyone around her was vigorously taking notes, keeping track of Ms. Healy's every word. It was funny—even the kids who took advanced classes broke down into subgroups. There were the super-straight preppies, which was her clan. But there were also the computer geeks who sat in the back of the class exchanging vintage comic books and CDs full of MP3s downloaded off the Internet by bands no one had ever heard of. They spent their lunch hours quoting old Monty Python movies and reading excerpts from cyberpunk novels like *Snow Crash.*

Then there were loners like Kara Doyle, "queen of the Goths," who wore the obligatory black hair, lipstick, and floor-length vintage dress, and who at this moment was passing a note to another loner, Ian Yates, who was into extreme BMX biking and cartoons. The way Ian unfolded the note, Madison could tell he and Kara were definitely into each other. Which brought up the truly big shadow that hung over Madison's fairly perfect life: no boyfriend.

Madison slumped in her seat. If loners like Kara and Ian could find each other, why couldn't she find her perfect mate? God! Even the Reverend Dimmesdale and Hester Prynne in *The Scarlet Letter* had found love. Of course, they got caught having an affair, so Hester had to wear that big red *A* for Adulteress for the rest of her life, and the reverend died of guilt and grief, but still . . .

Ding! The chime sounded on her PalmPilot, signaling that she had mail. Ms. Healy was startled by the sound and looked up from her lecture notes, an irritated look on her face. Madison quickly picked up her copy of *The Scarlet Letter* and made a show of looking extremely interested in what Ms. Healy was saying. It must have worked, because Ms. Healy looked back down at her notes and continued to drone on.

As Ian passed a note back to Kara, who tucked it into her black embroidered bag, Madison sneaked her PalmPilot out of her purse and tapped on the envelope icon. Could Blue have read her letter and written her back already? Yes!

Dear Pinky,
A tattoo? With needles and pain? Think I'll pass on that one. Though if I did get a tattoo, it would have to be a happy face with "Have a nice day!" written under it. Simple sentiment, but basically a good idea. Imagine if every day was a truly "nice" day.
    You realize you have given me two clues about your identity: You are

tattoo-less, and you are a junior.

Which is true of me, too. So far, we seem to be a perfect match. But just to confirm it, here are a few more factoids about me: I play the guitar but seriously doubt I'll ever make it into a band. I secretly write poetry to be shared with no one but me. Cats are fine, but I am definitely a total dog person. And although we live in this extremely wet, congested city, I have discovered some places in downtown Seattle that still qualify as— dare a guy say it?—lovely.

Oops, almost used the L word, gotta go!

Blue

Madison chuckled out loud. This guy was funny and romantic, and she liked him, whoever he was.

"Madison, have I said something amusing?"

Madison looked up to see Ms. Healy standing beside her desk.

"No, Ms. Healy," Madison answered meekly.

Ms. Healy was a no-nonsense teacher if there ever was one. If she had lived in New England during Puritan times, which was when the story of *The Scarlet Letter* took place, Madison was sure she would have been one of the mean old biddies who turned on Hester Prynne and forced her to wear that big red letter.

"Would you care to share with the rest of the class what is so funny?"

Madison gulped. Ms. Healy was staring hard at Madison's PalmPilot, which was absolutely forbidden in class, along with cell phones, CD players, and any other distracting electrical equipment.

Madison instantly started vamping. "Well, Ms. Healy, I was just musing on how ridiculous a scarlet letter would be today, and who would have to wear one—senators, actors, teachers, even a few of our presidents. In fact, there would probably be more people wearing the scarlet letter than not wearing it."

Ms. Healy's cold blue eyes looked huge through her extra-magnified glasses. "This is funny?"

Madison swallowed hard. "I guess it's really more ironic, wouldn't you say?"

Ms. Healy, who knew Madison as a straight-A, straight-shooter kind of student, softened a little. "'Ironic' is indeed the perfect word for it," she said with a brisk nod. "Now put the personal digital assistant away and pay attention, Ms. McKay."

As Ms. Healy walked back to the front of the room, Henry Cooney, Madison's partner in chem lab, mouthed the words, "Nice save."

Madison wiped some imaginary sweat off her forehead with her hand and tried to focus once again on the lecture. She forced herself to keep her eyes glued to Ms. Healy and soon found herself wondering what had turned the teacher into such an old grump. She was clearly smart and sometimes very funny, in a droll sort of way. Take away those awful glasses, let her hair out of that tight metal barrette at her neck, and Ms. Healy could almost be considered attractive. Maybe she'd had some brush with failed love that had made her go sour. Or worse yet—what if she had *never* had any brush with love at all, and this dried-up old prune was what Ms. Healy had become?

Madison swallowed hard. This could happen to her. She decided to make a resolution and share it with the one person who wouldn't tell.

The moment the bell rang, Madison tapped her vow into the PalmPilot.

Hey Blue,
I'm making a New Year's resolution—five months late. Since this qualifies as innermost thoughts, who better to share it with than you? My school and after-school commitments give me a pretty full schedule, which translates to zero love life. Not sure if it's really because of the full schedule or if I fill my schedule because I'm afraid that I might actually fall for someone and have to suffer through all that teenage heartbreak angst. ANYWAY, my vow is to not worry about the end but focus on the beginning, and be open to the L word.
Pinky
P.S. If I were to get a tattoo, it would say, "Bring it on!"

Madison hit SEND and grinned. Heart-2-Heart was a great program. She made a mental note to tell Mr. Wheeler that.

Madison stepped out of the classroom into the swirling mass of students all heading for their lockers and the school parking lot. It was like diving into a rushing river: You didn't try to fight against the current; you just kept your head above water and let the flow sweep you along.

"Yo, Madison!" Lou Garcia pushed his muscular bulk through the river of students with the same ease that he plowed through defensive linemen as the fullback on the Evergreen Eagles football team. "Reed Rawlings wanted me to be on his election team, but I told him no way, you had my vote."

Madison squeezed his arm, which was as thick as a tree trunk, and just as hard. "Thanks, Lou, that means a lot."

"I want to help," he said.

"What?" Madison could barely hear him over a trio of kids yelling the chorus to a song by The Ataris.

"I want to help," Lou repeated. "You know, be on your team or staff, or whatever you call it. That cool with you?"

"That's awesome!" Madison cried. Lou Garcia was one of the best-liked guys in school. Having him on her side in the big campaign was a major plus. Before she could say more, the Stafford twins, Dana and

Diana, grabbed her by the hand and turned her around as they moved the opposite way down the hall.

"Congratulations, Madison," Dana said. "You've got our vote!" Her sister bobbed her head up and down in enthusiastic agreement. Even at seventeen, the identical blondes still dressed alike, from the preppy tips of their loafers to the monogrammed *D*'s on their cardigan sweaters.

"Thanks, guys." Madison spun out of the circle and hurried to catch up with Lou. "Hey, Lou, did you really mean what you just said?"

Lou's broad face creased into a grin. "Affirmative."

"We're meeting at Giorgio's tomorrow night to power back pizza and brainstorm strategies for the campaign," she told him. "Want to come?"

"Seven o'clock, Giorgio's," Lou said, giving her a high five. "I'm there." Then he spied his locker and, with a wave good-bye, stepped out of the stream of students.

Madison continued forward with the crowd. She saw her locker ahead but she also saw what had to be a major roadblock:

Jeremy Drum, her new opponent and arch-nemesis. It didn't help that he was talking to her other rival.

Reed Rawlings spotted her before she could duck out of the flow of students. "Madison! This is too perfect. Join us."

Reed stood coolly in the middle of the hall, oblivious to the swarm of kids around him.

"Reed, I'd love to join you," Madison shouted above the bustle. "But I told Piper I'd meet her in the parking lot."

"This'll just take a minute," Reed insisted.

Madison hesitated. Much as she wanted to avoid talking to Jeremy, she didn't want to look like a rude jerk. She maneuvered her way around Jeremy and stood next to Reed.

"Of course you know Jeremy," Reed said, not letting her off the hook.

Jeremy answered for her. "We're like this," he said, holding up two fingers at arm's length.

"Funny," Madison replied without a smile.

Reed seemed oblivious to their awkwardness. "Listen up. My mom's a marketing specialist and she might be able to get us some airtime on some of the local radio stations. What do you think?"

Jeremy nodded. "That would be extremely cool."

"Would the interviews be separate?" Madison asked, not wanting to spend any time in close proximity to Jeremy. "I'd prefer to do mine alone—or with you, Reed."

Jeremy scowled. "What is it with you, Madison? Can't you at least be civil?"

"Not to you," Madison said with an angry toss of her head.

"Give me a break," Jeremy snapped.

"Whoa! Time out! Truce!" Reed quickly stepped between them and draped his arms around their shoulders. "Look, this is just an election. You don't need to get so malignant."

"Save the lecture for someone who needs it," Jeremy grumbled. "Like Miss Stuck-up."

Madison clutched her chest as if she'd been shot in the heart. "Oh, you got me," she said melodramatically. "I'm mortally wounded."

Jeremy's cheeks flared a deep red. Clenching his fists at his sides, he took several deep breaths. Clearly he was trying not to say anything back to Madison. At last he turned to Reed and said evenly, "The radio station idea is a good one. I'll catch you later to discuss it." He turned on his heel and strode away.

Madison felt the heat creep into her own face. Most of the students nearby had witnessed the entire exchange. Madison felt pretty certain that, at this moment, she looked like a complete, raving idiot.

Reed shook his head in amazement. "Wow. I don't need to do a thing to win this election," he said with a chuckle. "I'll just stand back and let you two destroy each other."

4

"**L**isten up, people!" Alex Kazinsky shouted over the music blasting from the speakers hanging from the ceiling.

It was Thursday night, and he and the rest of the Elect Madison Committee, as they now called themselves, had taken over half of Giorgio's Pizzeria. Alex and Lou Garcia had pushed four of the picnic tables—each covered with a red-and-white-checked tablecloth—into a big checkered square. Piper had recruited a few of the gang from the school newspaper, the *Eagle's Cry,* plus some well-chosen "brainiacs" from Honors English, to help fill out the brainstorming session.

As usual, Alex was a goofy sight. He

held court at the head of the table, a yellow pad in one hand and a pen with a green alien face that blinked on and off in the other. A huge red-and-white-striped *Cat in the Hat* cap perched on top of his flaming red hair. He twirled his pen like a small baton and declared, "Okay. Let's talk about the competition."

"That's easy." Piper took a bite of sausage pizza and kept chewing while she talked. "The competition is Reed Rawlings. He's rich, handsome, and smart."

"If he's so hot, why doesn't he have a girlfriend?" Liz Struthers asked as she dug a fork into her small chef salad. Liz, who could have won a Halle Berry look-alike contest, edited the *Eagle's Cry.* She epitomized classy elegance in her trademark black linen trousers, white starched shirt, and Marc Jacobs sandals.

"Is he taking applications?" Stacey Merrill called from the far end of the table. The spiky blonde had recently broken up with her longtime boyfriend, James Roland, for the umpteenth time.

"Tell me you're kidding," Lou Garcia said, stuffing his fifth piece of pizza in his mouth. He pulled a fistful of napkins from the dispenser and wiped them across his face. "Reed's a desperado. He's always scamming on the freshman girls."

"Hey!" Mouse protested in her high, squeaky voice. "I'm a freshman."

"Then you're just his type," Lou replied, tossing a wadded-up napkin in her direction.

"Careful, Mouse," computer whiz Henry Cooney warned. "Even freshmen get tired of hearing Reed talk about himself."

"Which is exactly why he has no girlfriend," Liz concluded.

Alex flipped the pen and began scribbling on the yellow pad. "So under Reed's name I'm writing 'rich and handsome but desperately lonely.'"

"Just a minute," Madison protested from her spot on the bench beside Alex. "You could write the same thing about me."

"Really?" Alex's eyes widened. "You're rich and handsome? Why, Maddy, you've been holding out on me." He cupped both hands around his mouth and shouted to the whole pizza parlor, "Put your money away. Miss Rich and Handsome is buying the pizza for everyone."

A rowdy cheer went up from several leather-jacketed guys in a corner booth.

Madison grabbed Alex's pen. "That's not what I meant!" Then she shouted toward the guys in the booth, "Delete that last comment from your memory bank. I'm not handsome, and in no way am I rich. Buy your own pizza!"

Liz Struthers leaned across the picnic table and asked coyly, "So what *did* you mean, Madison?"

Madison lowered her voice and said, in a confidential tone, "Well, I don't have a boyfriend. Does that make me desperately lonely?"

Liz raised an eyebrow. "You tell me."

"Now hold it!" Alex yanked his pen out of Madison's hand and waggled it at her. "It's not like you haven't had a zillion opportunities. Even I've been given the famous Madison McKay turndown." He took off his hat and hung his head in mock shame.

Madison stared at him in surprise. During their freshman and sophomore years, Alex had asked Madison out to a couple of dances, but she'd only turned him down because she'd already had a date. She'd always thought he'd understood. She had no idea he'd felt rejected.

"S'okay, Maddy. I forgive you," he said, and pounded her on the back. Madison was so startled that she snorted right out of her nose the cola she was sipping.

"Whoa!" Lou Garcia leaped back from the table and burst out laughing. "That's soooo presidential!"

This only made everyone laugh harder, including Madison. Mouse, who was normally pretty quiet, was giggling so much, she started to hiccup.

"All right, all right!" Alex shouted above the noise. He pounded a bottle of Parmesan cheese on the table like a gavel. "People! We need to stay focused."

"Geez, you guys," Madison said as she wiped the tears from her eyes. "If this is what our committee meetings are going to be like, I don't think I'm going to make it to Election Day."

"Election Day!" Piper warbled. "Way to bring us back to reality, Mad. One week from next Monday, the students at Evergreen High will cast their votes." She grabbed the Parmesan shaker from Alex and spoke into it like a microphone. "And now, Miss McKay, would you please tell this committee why anyone should vote for you?"

Madison took the shaker from Piper and spoke into it. "People like Mr. Kaufman say we're the hope for the future, the leaders of tomorrow—but he's wrong. As far as I'm concerned, the so-called leaders of today are screwing things up pretty royally. Our future begins now. We need to take the lead, now."

"And how, Ms. McKay, are we going to do that?" asked Liz.

"We start by reaching out to the community. Join forces to make change happen. I've already talked to people at several community action programs, like the Fremont InterUrban Shelter Group and the Neighborhood Network of Puget Sound, and they are way pumped for Evergreen High to get on board and help. Even if I don't win, I'm going to pursue this."

Lou slammed a fist on the table. "Madison's got game."

"Madison is bank," Alex agreed. The second he said that, his eyes widened, and he quickly wrote it down on his yellow pad.

"What else? We're looking for the really big slogan. You know, the one that we print on the buttons. Come on, people—think!"

Mouse leaped up and squeaked, "How about, 'Go all the way with Madison McKay'?"

Everyone gave her a shocked look, and she immediately sat down. "Oops. Not a good idea."

Alex consulted his yellow pad again. "While you're thinking, put this in your cranial hopper. Reed has more money than God. He can do great giveaways. How do we compete with that?"

"Excuse me?" Liz dabbed at the corners of her mouth with her napkin and pushed her salad bowl away. "But Reed is not our competition in this race."

Piper stopped in the middle of taking a drink of her iced tea. "Come on," she scoffed. "You can't think Jeremy's got any sort of chance?"

Liz shrugged. "I thought his speech was pretty good. It sure hit home with a lot of kids."

"Just the lowlifes and losers," Stacey said, fiddling with one of the pierced studs on her upper ear. "That's a very small percentage of the student body."

"That's not true," Madison said. As much as she loathed Jeremy Drum for what he'd done to her, she had to admit that his speech had been a good one. "I heard the applause. It came from a lot of people." Madison could see from the looks on their faces that everyone at the table agreed with her. "But we all know what a jerk he is, so it's up to us to spread the word."

Lou pushed up the sleeves on his rugby shirt. "Am I missing something here? I've got Jeremy in a couple of my classes and, frankly, he seems like a pretty cool guy. Kind of a loner, maybe, but he can be a real crack-up."

Piper and Alex exchanged looks.

"You guys, Lou doesn't know," Liz said quietly. "He wasn't here our freshman year."

"Know what?" Lou asked. "Is this some kind of secret?"

Madison shook her head. "It's no secret, Lou. It's just embarrassing. For me."

Piper put her hand on Madison's arm. "Let me tell it. I was in the bleachers, watching." She lowered her voice and started the story. "It was at Homecoming our freshman year. As you know, Evergreen High elects a Homecoming queen and her court. There's a princess from each class."

Lou looked at Madison. "Were you the freshman princess?"

"Yes," Madison replied, then covered her face with her hands. "I mean, no. I wasn't. But I *thought* I was."

Mouse, who wasn't at the school then, either, asked, "But how did that happen?"

Madison squeezed her eyes shut as the events of that awful night came rushing back to her in vivid detail. She and Piper were there in the stands with a bunch of friends from the float committee. All of them were thrilled to be at their very first Homecoming game. Their class had built the royal float, which had carried the football players onto the field earlier that evening. Now it would carry the royal court. She remembered how proud she had felt of her work on the float, and how proud she was to be a student at Evergreen High.

It was a particularly cold night. They'd huddled under the wool blankets Piper's mom had sent with them, but they were still cold.

"At halftime," Piper explained to the group, "Madison offered to run to get us hot chocolates. She said she'd go to the Visitor's side to get them because the line would be shorter. We all thought that was brilliant."

Madison remembered stepping into the tunnel that led to the concession stands under the bleachers. She passed the Stafford twins, in their matching green-and-white stocking caps and scarves. They were standing in line on the "Home" side. Reed Rawlings was in front of the twins, and next to him was a guy in a leather jacket and dark green stocking cap. That guy was Jeremy Drum, a recent transfer from Garfield High. When he saw Madison he smiled and waved. So did Reed. Madison remembered thinking at the time how odd it was that Reed and Jeremy were standing next to each other. Both of them had asked her to the game.

Madison hurried to buy her hot chocolates and as she was returning to the "Home" side, she heard the halftime festivities begin. It was agonizing. She could barely hear the announcer's muffled voice under the bleachers.

Madison's thoughts were interrupted as

she heard Piper say, "While Madison was buying the hot chocolate, the announcer explained that players from the football team would be coming into the stands to identify the royal court and escort them to the float."

"Which girls made the Homecoming court?" Mouse asked.

"Kira Kelly was the queen that year. Danielle Austin was junior princess. Zoe Elderman was sophomore princess—"

Madison finished for her. "And the freshman princess was McKenzie Madsen."

Lou Garcia had been listening to Piper with his arms crossed on the table. He leaned forward and murmured, "I think I'm beginning to understand the confusion. But how does Jeremy fit into the picture?"

Madison stared hard at the red-and-white checks on the tablecloth. She remembered the next part of the story in vivid detail. The names were announced over the PA system, but she couldn't hear any of them clearly. However, the last name had sounded an awful lot like hers. She tried to pick up her pace to get back to the field, but the cups of hot chocolate slowed her down.

Just as she reached the entrance back into the stadium, Jeremy appeared. He seemed genuinely excited. "Madison!" he yelled. "It's you! Get out there!"

"You're kidding!" Madison had squealed in delight. She spun in a frantic circle trying to figure out what to do with the cups of hot chocolate. Reed was in line at the drink stand, but a lot of kids were crowded around the entrance to the stadium.

Madison couldn't remember if Reed had offered to hold the drinks for her or if she just handed them to him, but she did remember suddenly being pulled through the crowd behind Jeremy as he shouted, "'Scuse me! 'Scuse me! Let the princess through!"

The Stafford twins parted to let Jeremy and Madison pass. Thinking back on it for the trillionth time, Madison should have known something was not right because Dana and Diana had given her funny looks. Normally they would have been all over her, squealing and jumping up and down. But at that moment Madison had been too excited to think straight.

"Go!" Jeremy said, pushing her forward. "Run out there! To the float!"

Madison winced and put her face in her hands as Piper described what happened next.

"The crowd went wild as the royal court came out of the stands," Piper told the others. "Spotlights swirled all over the bleachers looking for the winners, and then the lights followed them as they made their way to the float. All at once, the cheering stopped, as if everyone had inhaled at once."

"I remember that moment," Liz whispered. "It was surreal."

"What happened?" Mouse whispered back.

Piper looked over at Madison, whose hands were still covering her face. "Do you want me to tell it?"

Madison peeked between her fingers. "Go ahead. But be quick. It's still too awful to bear."

Piper nodded. "All of the winners were being crowned on the float, when another person appeared on the field. A spotlight picked her up and followed her all the way to the float."

Madison lowered her hands and looked up. "I heard the crowd gasp, but I didn't know what was wrong. And when the spot-light shone on me, I assumed it was because I had won. So I kept on running to join the others, waving and grinning like a goon."

"Ouch," Lou Garcia said, wincing.

"I still didn't get it until I ran up the steps and joined the winners on the float. There I was, face-to-face with McKenzie Madsen. She was wearing the crown, and I was wearing——"

"Huevos rancheros," Alex finished for her.

"What did you do?" Mouse asked. "I would have curled up and died."

Madison laughed for the first time since the story had begun. "I wanted to die, believe me. But I did the first thing that came into my head."

"It was so great. She did an about face," Piper said, "saluted the crowd and ran back down the steps and off the field."

"And *that's* the moment when I curled up and died," Madison explained to Mouse. "I think I cried for a whole month."

Madison remembered her tears blinding her before she'd reached the exit. She lived three miles away and had run the entire way home. All she'd wanted to do was go to bed for the rest of her life.

"I hope you got Jeremy good for that one," Lou said grimly.

Piper pushed her glasses up on her nose. "For a while we didn't know what had happened. Madison wouldn't take any phone calls or see anybody."

Liz tapped a long painted fingernail on Lou's arm. "When we heard that Jeremy was the one who had lied to her and shoved her onto the field, everyone—"

"And she does mean *everyone*—," Piper emphasized.

"Cut Jeremy dead," Liz finished. "Even the teachers."

During the story, Henry Cooney had been quietly tearing a paper napkin into little tiny strips. He looked up and said, "Did anyone ever ask Jeremy why he did it?"

"It was obvious," Alex said with a shrug. "Revenge. He wanted to go to Homecoming with Madison, but she turned him down."

Madison frowned at her friend. "It wasn't a turndown," she protested. "I just told him I had already made plans with Piper and the others on the Float Committee. I invited him to join us. He seemed fine with that."

Alex raised his flashing alien pen. "Ah, he *seemed* to understand. Who knows what deeper, darker motive drove him to humiliate you?"

Henry scooped his shredded napkin into a neat white pile in front of him. "Maybe it was a mistake. Maybe he thought he heard Madison's name being called."

"If that was the case," Piper said, "the guy could have apologized. But he didn't."

Liz nodded in agreement. "And when people eventually asked him why he did it, he just got all gnarly and told them to leave him alone."

Madison raised her hand. "You guys, can we stop? I don't think I can stand another minute of this humiliating trip down Memory Lane."

Alex stood up. "Right. As my great-uncle Seymour always said, 'If it doesn't kill you, it'll only make you stronger.'" Alex lifted his glass of root beer in a toast. "Here's to Maddy—the strongest person I know!"

Madison raised her glass and toasted with the others.

Mouse took a swig of her root beer and then said, "I just have one last question.

What happened to the hot chocolates?"

Piper put her hands on her hips. "Good question. We certainly never got to drink them. I'll bet Jeremy took them."

"Or Reed," Liz reminded the others, "After all, he was the one who took them from Madison at the drink stand."

"Then Rawlings owes me," Madison joked, reaching for another slice of pizza. "Next time I see him, I'm going to make him pay up."

"With interest!" Piper added.

Madison munched happily on her pizza and took a moment to bask in the warmth of this gathering of her friends. As unpleasant as it was to remember those horrible events from two years before, the process made her realize how far she had come.

At the time, Madison had really thought her social life at Evergreen High was over. How wrong she'd been! Her natural optimism and spirit had come back in full force. She'd thrown herself into the life of the school and had really made an effort to put the Homecoming disaster and Jeremy behind her. Now here she was, two years later, making a serious run for school president!

5

Dear Blue,

Uh-oh. Just got back from a meeting, and what was the first thing I did when I came through the front door? Checked to see if there was a message from you. This Heart-2-Heart thing is getting to be addictive. We had pizza at the meeting. My fave is Canadian bacon and pineapple. We had sausage. Boo. The meeting was fun, but I would rather have been riding the ferry out to Bainbridge Island at sunset, or strolling through Pike Place Market watching those goofy fish sellers crack jokes while they juggle tuna and salmon.

As I write this a fly just buzzed past me and has now landed upside down on the ceiling—which brings me to the burning question for this evening: How do they do that?

And as long as I'm asking burning questions—what do you look like? I'm curious.
                                        Pinky

Madison hit SEND on her keyboard and
leaned back in her desk chair. She'd positioned her deep red mahogany writing desk
next to her bedroom window because she
loved the view so much. Madison lived with
her parents and younger brother, Sean, in a
rambling old Victorian house on top of
Queen Anne Hill in the heart of Seattle.

From her window, which faced south,
Madison could see the towering high-rise
buildings downtown, punctuated by the
gleaming spire of the Space Needle. Then
there was the long, sweeping arc of the
waterfront and the ferryboat terminal at
Elliott Bay, bordering the deep blue waters
of Puget Sound. The Sound was dotted with
freighters and the familiar green and white
ferryboats as they cruised back and forth
between Seattle and the islands to the west.
Ringing the entire view was a great, long
border of snowcapped mountains. Of course,
Seattle was usually overcast, so those mountains were often hidden by gray clouds. But

on sunny days, there was no view more spec-
tacular, especially when Mount Rainier rose
out of the clouds like a giant ice-cream cone.

It was night now, and she could see the
lights on a ferryboat coming in from the
islands. She imagined herself standing at
the ferryboat railing, with Blue at her side.
He'd have his arm around her, holding her
close, protecting her from the wind. Chilled,
she'd bury her face in his chest, then tilt her
chin up to look in his—brown? blue?—
eyes. He'd be taller than she was, of course.
Then he'd lower his face to hers and gently
plant a kiss on her glossy lips.

Ding! The computer signaled that she
had mail.

Madison shook her head and turned
away from the glittering lights of Seattle
and checked the in-box on her e-mail program. Was it from Blue? Yes!

Dear Curious Pinky,
If I told you what I looked like, then
I'd lose my status as your secret
admirer, which is what I'm becoming
as I read your messages. Any girl who
likes Ben & Jerry's ice cream, sun-

sets on Puget Sound, and fish guys who juggle tuna can't be all bad. I have to draw the line at pineapple on pizza, but I'm sure there are other food groups we can share.

We could also hit the waterfront, feed the seagulls, and visit my favorite—Ye Olde Curiosity Shop at Pier 54. Let's skip the seashell ashtrays and plastic Space Needle souvenirs in front and go straight to the back. We'll peek through a magnifying glass and see two fleas dressed up as a bride and groom, or read an entire poem written on a single grain of rice. Then we'll gawk at the mummified remains of Sylvester the old prospector found in the Arizona desert one hundred years ago.

I wonder about many things, too—like what color your eyes are, and what your voice might sound like?

Blue

P.S. A fly grabs the ceiling with little suction cups on its front legs, then flips its back legs over to catch the ceiling. When I was nine, I learned to

do a backflip off my cousin's diving
board in Issaquah, but I cannot do
that.

Madison chuckled out loud as she read
Blue's note. Whoever this guy was, she liked
him. A lot. She scooted her chair close to her
desk and immediately typed a reply.

Dear Wondering Blue,

My eyes are brown. I guess that doesn't give away
my identity, but it does narrow the field. It means
that I cannot possibly be Liz Struthers, with her
huge hazel green eyes, or Jill Klein, with her not-
of-this-world-blue contacts. And I think the
Stafford twins have gray eyes, but I can't be certain about it.

I have never actually thought about the
sound of my voice. When I sing in the shower, I
think I sound terrific, but my brother (clue!) would
disagree. Confession: You know how, in movies,
when they want to show the mom finally bonding
with her daughters, or the football team finally
pulling together just before the Big Game, they
always sing "Ain't No Mountain High Enough"
while jumping on the bed in their underwear, or
slapping one another with towels in the locker

room? Well, I have done that. I put on the song, grab a hairbrush or my brother's Mister Mike, and sing at the top of my lungs—in front of my mirror. Of course, I don't bond with anyone—least of all, my brother. And as long as I'm confessing, I have also stood in front of my mirror with tears streaming down my face, just to see if I cry beautifully.

I have never been inside Ye Olde Curiosity Shop, but I know where it is because we've driven by those huge totem poles out front a zillion times. I'd like to see the fleas, but not sure about the mummified prospector. Would like to do the Underground Seattle tour. It's only a few blocks from Pier 54 to Pioneer Square. We can hop on a trolley down Alaskan Way, and then walk from there.

Thanks for the information about the fly. My life is better, knowing that. Someday you must show me your backflip and I'll show you my jack-knife, which I learned to do in diving lessons at Girl Scout camp. Yes, I was a Girl Scout. Want to buy a cookie?

Pinky

Bam. Bam. Bam. Madison's twelve-year-old brother, Sean, was pounding on her bedroom door. "Madison!"

Madison quickly hit SEND and went to answer her door. Sean was leaning against the wall, completely engrossed in the Good Charlotte CD he was listening to on his Walkman. Madison knew it was Good Charlotte because Sean had the volume cranked up so high, she could hear the music right through the earphones.

"Mom wants to know what's going on," her brother shouted extra loudly. "She hasn't seen you since breakfast."

"Um . . ." Madison looked back at her computer. She didn't want to leave. What if Blue wrote back? She didn't want to miss his letter. "Tell Mom I'll be down in a minute."

Sean, who was bobbing his head in time with the music, shouted, "What?"

Madison lifted one of his earphones and said, "I'll be down in a minute. Tell Mom that."

Sean shook his head. "No go. She wants to see you now. And I'm not coming back."

Madison stepped through her door into the hall, making sure to close the door behind her. The last thing she needed was her younger brother reading her e-mails. "Where is she?"

"In the library, watching the History Channel," Sean replied. He trotted down the stairs ahead of her and peeled off to the left toward the family room. Madison passed through the front hall into the room filled with floor-to-ceiling bookcases. Her mother was sitting in one of the caramel brown leather wingback chairs, doing a crossword puzzle while she watched TV.

Madison perched across from her on the edge of the matching leather chair. "Hi, Mom. What did you need?"

Mrs. McKay took off her reading glasses and flicked off the TV with the remote. "I just wanted to know how the Big Day went. After all that hectic preparation yesterday, and then the Election Committee meeting this evening at Giorgio's, you haven't said a word about it. What's up?"

Madison gave her mother a quick rundown of the last two days' events, tossing in some funny stories about Alex Kazinsky at the pizza parlor, and glossing over the surprise entry of Jeremy Drum into the presidential race the day before. Then she stood up, anxious to get back to her computer. "May I have some money?" she asked as she backed out of the library. "I need to buy some art supplies for the election. You know, poster board, paints, stuff like that."

"Of course," her mom replied. "But what's your hurry? You came in the front door and went straight to your room. Now you're going back?"

"Oh, I'm working on an assignment for my advisory group," she explained. "And it involves e-mailing some of my, um, work partners."

"Okay, honey," her mother said, slipping her glasses back on her nose. "But don't work too hard. It's getting late."

"Okay." Madison took the stairs two at a time. As she threw open her bedroom door, the phone began to ring and her heart skipped a beat. What if it was Blue? He'd said he wanted to hear her voice. She grabbed the receiver. "Hello?"

"Hi, Mad," Piper's voice sang out in her ear.

"Oh, it's you," Madison said, falling back on the pink brocade duvet covering her double bed.

"Of course it's me. I always call you at this time," Piper said. "Who'd you think it was?"

"I thought you were Blue," she said with

a giggle. "But that's, of course, impossible, since Blue doesn't even know my name."

"Just what are you talking about?" Piper demanded. "And who is Blue?"

"Blue"—Madison grabbed one of her pink furry pillows that lined her headboard and hugged it to her chest—"is my Heart-2-Heart partner. And I think I'm in love."

"What!" Piper screeched into the phone. "We were just assigned our partners yesterday. I have spent almost every spare minute with you, except for a few hours last night and the two hours since we left Giorgio's. When could you possibly have found the time to fall in love?"

"Okay," Madison said, rolling over onto her stomach. "Maybe not love with a capital L. But a very strong like. Blue is funny and smart—he knows how flies land on the ceiling upside down. And talented—he can do a backflip. Or at least he could when he was nine at his cousin's house in Issaquah."

"He put all that in one letter?" Piper asked.

Madison giggled. "Of course not. We've e-mailed several letters. In fact, I'm expecting one now."

"Geez," Piper said a little wistfully. "I haven't even checked to see if my Heart-2-Heart pal wrote back."

Madison plucked at the fuzzy strands of yarn on her pillow. "You should. I love this program! We can tell each other *anything*. It's so great!"

"And this guy's name is Blue?" Piper's voice sounded doubtful. "I don't remember any kid at school named Blue. There was that one guy we called Green in our chem lab, remember? But I think we called him that because his last name *was* Green and we could never remember his first name."

Madison giggled even more. She was feeling like a fizzy soda pop, bubbly all over. "Oh, Piper, his name isn't really Blue. That's just his nickname."

"Do you have a nickname?"

"Of course," Madison said. "But I don't want to tell you what it is. You'll think it's ridiculous."

"I can't believe you won't tell me," Piper protested. "I'm your BFF. We share everything!"

"I know. . . ."

"Come on, tell me!" Piper pleaded.

"Look, I told you about the time I wet my pants in second grade, and that I had a total crush on Mr. Proctor, our fifth-grade teacher. And last year, when I—"

"This is different, Piper," Madison tried to explain. "We can tell our deepest secrets to our Heart-2-Heart pal because they don't know who we are."

"I just can't believe this," Piper continued in a really hurt voice. "Didn't I tell you about that D I almost got in Algebra I and the secret tutor I had to hire to bring up my grade? God, I even told you about that mole on my butt that I had to have removed. If that's not a deep secret, I don't know what is."

"Okay, okay!" Madison sat up. "I'll tell you. It's Pinky."

There was a long pause. "Pinky? That's ridiculous."

"See!" Madison shouted into the phone. "I knew you'd say that." She got up and crossed to her vanity mirror. She tousled her hair with one hand to make it stand up. "It had to do with dyeing my hair pink."

There was an even longer pause.

"You're not going to do that, are you?"

Piper asked quietly. "Because I don't think it will help the campaign. Oh, it might steal a few votes from Jeremy—but do we really need them? I'm not sure."

"Piper, relax," Madison said. "I was just joking about doing it."

Ding! The computer sounded across the room, signaling the arrival of another e-mail.

"It's him!" Madison squealed, spinning to look at her computer. "Listen, Piper, I can't talk now. Blue just wrote me a note."

"Hold it! You're hanging up on your best friend just so you can read an e-mail from some random guy named Blue?" Piper huffed. "You don't really know anything about him. And he could be making all sorts of stuff up."

"He's nice," Madison protested.

"Oh, yeah? What if you find out that 'Blue' is actually Leonard Watkins, number one freak-a-zoid at EHS?"

Madison winced at the thought. Leonard was certainly strange to look at—barely five feet tall, with oversized glasses, bad skin, and hair that looked like steel wool. But that was just looks. "Maybe Leonard is a nice guy.

I know he lurks around the halls humming to himself, but you know, if he really was 'Blue,' I'd give him a chance."

"You're certifiably insane," Piper declared. "You have all these guys at Evergreen High drooling over you and you fall for some unknown named Blue. Hmm . . . if that's the way to get guys, maybe I'd better hang up and check my e-mail. Some maniac named Lemon Yellow could have sent me a letter that will change my life."

"Go for it, Piper!" Madison chuckled. "I'll see you tomorrow."

"Okay," Piper said. "Although I may have eloped to Vancouver with Lemon Yellow by then."

"Ciao!" Madison hung up the phone and leaped over her bed to get to her desk. She clicked on the letter icon and a message came up. But not from Blue.

Dear Madison,
I've got good news and bad news. The good news: We've got an interview with Kasey Kramer at KYXX radio on Saturday. The bad news: It's at 6 a.m. You can

thank me over breakfast after—
ward.

Truly yours,
Reed

Madison read the last line of Reed's letter over again. He was acting as if they were going out. Some girls, like Mouse or Stacey Merrill, would have been thrilled to get a note like this from Reed, but frankly, it left her cold. And a little down.

This was not the boy she wanted to hear from. She glanced at the digital clock on her bedside table. It was almost midnight. Blue had probably gone to bed. Maybe she would hear from him tomorrow morning.

Madison changed into her cloud-covered flannel pj bottoms and a white tee, and slipped under the covers of her down comforter. As she drifted off to sleep, images of Leonard Watkins and Reed Rawlings humming together with a mysterious figure cloaked in blue swirled in her head.

6

Madison checked the clock above the counter at Jitters coffee shop. Five forty-five A.M. Too early for anyone in her right mind to be up, especially on a Saturday. How could she ever have agreed to this? She felt puffy and achy. Her eyes were red-rimmed from lack of sleep. To make matters worse, just before she stumbled out of her house into the dark, Madison had checked her e-mail and Blue still hadn't written back. It had been nearly thirty-six hours since she'd sent him her note.

Madison took a sip of her mocha latte and wondered if maybe she'd shared a little too much—especially the part about watching herself cry. She winced just thinking about it.

"Jerk alert!" Piper's voice cut into Madison's thoughts like a shrill alarm clock.

"Where?" Madison nearly wrenched her neck trying to turn around in the booth.

"He's at the front door," Piper said without moving her lips. "Don't look. He'll think you care."

"But I do care," Madison said, holding a forced smile on her face. "Just not in a good way."

Both girls sat frozen, their hands clutching their cups of coffee as Jeremy Drum shuffled to the counter of the coffee shop. "Coffee. Black," he rumbled in a very deep voice. "To go."

"He sounds like he just woke up," Piper whispered.

"And looks like it, too," Madison said. "Do you think he slept in his clothes?"

Jeremy was wearing jeans, a wrinkled white T-shirt, and his ever-present black sport coat. His jet-black hair, which was always pretty unruly, was flat on one side and a rat's nest on the other.

Madison was the complete opposite. She had allowed herself a full hour to wash and blow-dry her hair, put on makeup, and dress for the interview on the *Good Morning, Seattle* radio program. Although she had that weird buzzy feeling like she'd stayed up all night, every hair was in place, and her pink-and-burgundy-striped turtleneck sweater matched exactly her pink-striped leg warmers and burgundy silk mini.

"I thought they were going to interview the presidential candidates separately," Madison murmured as she took another sip of her latte. "If I'd known Jeremy Drum was going to be here, I wouldn't have come."

Piper peered at Madison over today's pair of lime green oval glasses. "You hate Jeremy so much that you'd give up a spot on *Good Morning, Seattle*?"

Madison pursed her lips in thought. How long could she hold on to her grudge? It had been over two years since the Homecoming disaster, and any feelings of active hate really had faded. But, still . . .

"Let's just say, the less time I spend with Jeremy," she whispered, "the better."

Piper reached across the table and squeezed her arm. "Just stay cool. You're a shoo-in for president, and don't forget it. Jeremy is so *not* right for the job."

At that moment, the glass door swung open and in sauntered Reed Rawlings, looking crisp and businesslike in a blue corduroy blazer and cotton suede twills. He carried a leather briefcase.

"What about Reed?" Madison asked.

Piper rolled her eyes. "Puh-leeze. Reed is like some kind of country club wannabe. Nobody wants that for our school president."

"Well, at least he cares about the school," Madison countered. "Whereas Jeremy is the major slacker candidate."

The girls watched Jeremy give Reed a high-five hello. They were both handsome guys—Jeremy in a rumpled sort of way, and Reed in a very *GQ* way.

"'Scuse me, miss!" Reed called loudly to the girl behind the counter. "Could you get me a latte, pronto? I've got a big interview with Kasey Kramer on *Good Morning, Seattle* in a few minutes and I don't want to be late."

Piper rolled her eyes. "Did he rehearse that line, like, twenty times? He acts as if he's the only one being interviewed."

Madison, who was still watching Jeremy, murmured, "I wish he was."

"Get a grip, girlfriend," Piper said, snapping up her lime green car coat over her black cargo shorts and bright red tights. "Let's get out of here. If we beat them to the radio station, you can go first."

Piper adjusted her bright red beret and headed for the door. Madison hung back, taking extra time to gather her election materials in the slim hope that Jeremy and Reed might leave Jitters before she did. No such luck.

Madison looped her maroon nylon pack over her shoulder and strode purposefully toward the coffee-shop door.

"Hey, McKay!" Jeremy waved, clearly making an effort to be friendly. "Early enough for you?"

This was Madison's chance to be civil, but she just couldn't find it in her. "It's fine for me. I even found the time to brush my hair and get dressed."

Jeremy took a step back and held out both arms. "What am I? Naked?"

Reed leaned forward and whispered in an extra-loud voice, "I believe she is referring to your creased tee and extreme case of bed-head."

Jeremy didn't even flinch. "It's radio," he cracked. "Who cares what we look like?"

"*She* cares," Reed said, pointing to Madison as she pulled open the glass door.

"Too much, if you ask me," Jeremy replied, taking a swig of his coffee and looking her straight in the eye.

Madison wanted to shout back, "Who asked you!" but a group of chattering women came through the door, blocking her way. She waited until they had passed, but by then Jeremy had turned away, so she marched out the door.

There was a grain of truth in what Jeremy had said. Why *did* she care so much? Getting up an hour and a half before a radio interview just to make sure your hair looked perfect would be considered excessive in anyone's book. She glanced at the maroon portfolio that she'd tucked under her arm. Inside were her "talking points" for the interview. Was that excessive too?

"Come on, Maddy," Piper said, looping her arm through her friend's and hurrying her down the sidewalk to the radio station next door. "Let's get there first."

Madison had expected the radio station to be located in some impressive office building. To her surprise, the station wasn't much bigger than the tiny coffee place they'd just left. Two large plate-glass windows looked out onto the street. Through one she could see an immense, bearded man in headphones talking into a microphone. He sat behind a console lined with flashing electronic lights and switches. The other window revealed a cramped reception area with black leather chairs and a pretty blond receptionist sitting at a chrome-and-glass desk.

The receptionist greeted the girls and told them to take a seat next to the door marked RECORDING STUDIO. A red light was lit above the door, indicating that the radio show was "on the air."

Madison sat down, but her forehead was still creased in a frown from thinking about what Jeremy had said. Piper waved her hand in front of her face. "Hello? Excuse me? We've got a really important interview here, and you are becoming a total space case."

"Would you call me 'excessive'?" Madison asked Piper.

"Not to your face," Piper replied. "And, like, where did that come from?"

"I care about what I wear and what I say," Madison continued. "Would you call that excessive?"

Piper exhaled loudly and put a hand on Madison's arm. "You are the most organized person I know. You take notes about taking notes, which could be called excessive. But that's what will make you a great president of our school. You keep your eye on the details."

At that moment the speaker above their heads blared, "Good morning, Seattle! It's a great day here in the Emerald City. And what a shocker—not a cloud in the sky. This is Kasey Kramer, and have I got a treat for you listeners out there today. Three of Seattle's finest—and no, I'm not talking about cups of coffee—will be joining me here in the KYXX studios in just a few moments, right after we catch up with Jennifer Handley up in our eye-in-the-sky chopper. So tell us, Jen, what's the traffic like out there?"

A woman's voice began to report on an accident on I-5 near the Aurora Bridge, and how to avoid the congestion backing up traffic in the Denny Regrade.

Suddenly the recording studio door swung open, and a hugely overweight man in a black KYXX T-shirt and faded jeans stepped into the reception area. He held up a coffee mug and called out, "Nurse? Oh, nurse? I need a transfusion, but quick!"

The receptionist grabbed the man's coffee mug and hurried over to the coffeemaker. Madison whispered to Piper, "*That's* Kasey Kramer? He sounds so suave and handsome on the radio, and looks so—"

"Bulging biker-boy in person," Piper finished for her.

Luckily the DJ hadn't heard them. He was too busy shaking hands with Jeremy and Reed, who had just come into the reception area. Kasey grabbed his coffee and gestured for all of them to join him in the studio. "All right, troops, into the transporter room."

"All of us, at once?" Madison squeaked.

"The more the merrier," Kasey replied. "Now hurry up. Jennifer will be finished with the traffic report in"—he cocked one eye at a clock on the wall—"fifteen seconds."

Piper squeezed Madison's hand and said, "I'll wait for you. Rock their socks off, babe!"

Once inside the tiny recording booth, Kasey had each of them sit on a stool around the microphone while he slipped on his headphones. Madison pointedly sat next to Reed so she wouldn't be beside Jeremy. Unfortunately, that put her directly across from Jeremy, with her face only inches from his.

He blinked his big blue eyes at her, and for half a second Madison's pulse quickened. She'd spent so many years despising him that she'd forgotten how handsome he was. She started to smile, but Jeremy looked away quickly.

"Good morning, Seattle!" Kasey called into the microphone. "I'm sitting here in the driver's seat at KYXX, and my passengers on this wild ride are America's hope for the future. That's right, Evergreen High has sent over three of its finest to share some of their wisdom with you listeners. So let's give it up for Madison McKay, Jeremy Drum, and Reed Rawlings."

Kacey hit a button on his console, and a recording of cheers and whistles played over the studio monitors.

When the cheering stopped, Kasey spoke into his mike once more. "These beautiful people are all running for student body president at Evergreen High. So let's just dive in. Madison. Why do you think you should be president?"

Madison quickly flipped open her folder to her list of talking points. "Well, Kasey, I was president of our sophomore and junior class, I'm presently an officer in the Spanish Club—"

"Whoa, whoa, whoa!" Kasey cut her off. "That's just a résumé. What I want to hear—and I'm sure our listeners do too—is what you're going to bring to the table. How will you lead these stars of tomorrow forward?"

The abrupt interruption flustered Madison, and it took her a moment to regain her poise. "Um, Kasey, I-I don't want to sound like I'm just listing off past achievements," she stammered. "But I do feel my experience is a strong part of what I bring to the table.

I sit on a lot of committees and I'm used to listening to and working with others. My vision for our school is simple: Reach out, not just to other students at the school, but to others in the community. I'd like to develop more opportunities for us to make a difference in the world around us. We don't have to wait until we graduate to become leaders. We can begin right now."

Kasey Kramer nodded his head in approval. "Good answer. Reed, what about you?"

The entire time Madison was speaking, Reed had been frantically riffling through his briefcase. So when Kasey called on him, he said, "Kasey, I prepared a speech but, er, I'm having a little difficulty finding it."

"I can see why," Kasey replied with a laugh. He took Reed's case from his lap. "Folks, you should see what this guy has in his briefcase. Twenty 'Reed Will Lead' buttons. At least fifty 'We Need Reed' pencils. And what's this? 'Reed Rawlings' playing cards with a different picture of him on each card. That is way cool."

"My mom thought of that one," Reed chuckled. "She's a marketing director."

Kasey handed Reed's case back to him and said, "Well, Reed, speech or no speech, you are some kind of promotional beast."

"Thanks, Kasey," Reed said, taking the DJ's remark as a compliment. He opened his mouth to say more, but Kasey had already moved on.

"Last but not least, we have Jeremy Drum. So, Jeremy, do you have a briefcase full of fun giveaways to sway the voters your way?"

Jeremy shook his head. "No, I don't. Not one button or pencil."

"So what do you bring to the table?" Kasey asked.

"Just me." Jeremy tilted his head to look straight at the interviewer. "I bring me— the guy in the back of the class. The guy at the top of the bleachers. The guy on the sidelines at the dance."

"Yeah?" All at once Kasey Kramer looked genuinely interested. "So who is that guy?"

Jeremy shrugged. "That guy is Everyman. There is a small inside circle of students who do everything at Evergreen, and a giant circle of those on the outside who'd like to do something but are not sure how.

I'd like to invite them to the party, and include *everyone* in the life of the school. And I think we need to make those changes to our school first before we set out to change the world."

Kasey nodded in silence. Then he turned to his mike and said quietly, "You know, I was one of those guys in high school. The invisible ones at the top of the bleachers, looking for a way to fit in. More power to you, man." The DJ gave Jeremy a thumbs-up, then punched a button on his console. As hard-driving music began to play, Kasey said brightly, "There you have it, folks. The best and brightest from Seattle's own Evergreen High School. *Good Morning, Seattle* salutes our leaders of tomorrow. And now, today's headlines."

Kasey took the next three minutes to read the news. Madison sat with her head bent, thinking about what Jeremy had said. She'd always been the kid at the front of the room, and had just assumed those in the back of the class were there because they wanted to be there. It was something to think about. When she raised her head, she found herself looking directly into Jeremy's eyes again. This time he didn't look away. She couldn't tell what she saw in his steady gaze. Indifference?

After the news, Kasey spoke into the mike again. "I want to thank you three for coming by this morning. In a little over a week, students at Evergreen High will cast their votes and one of these fine young people will be their new leader." He turned to look at the three candidates. "We've got about one more minute of airtime before I release you from this loony bin. Time enough for each of you to send one final message to the people of Seattle and the students of Evergreen High."

Kasey pointed to them one at a time, and they leaned toward the mike to say good-bye. Reed went first. "Thanks—and remember, a vote for Reed means we all will succeed." He pumped his fist toward the microphone, and his briefcase slipped off his lap, scattering the contents all over the floor. "My stuff!"

As Reed picked up his pencils and banners, Jeremy leaned in to the mike and said, "Rock on, Evergreen High!"

Madison took a deep breath. "I'll close with Gandhi's words: 'Be the change you want to see in the world.'"

Kasey flipped a switch, and a water bed commercial began to play. He rolled his office chair over to the studio door and held it open. As Madison, Jeremy, and Reed hurried out of the tiny studio back into the reception area, Kasey called after them, "Thanks again for coming, and good luck in your campaigns!"

He shut the door, and the interview was over. Reed shook his head. "Wow, that was short."

"Yeah," Jeremy chuckled. "If the audience tuned out for a second, they missed us."

They found Piper doubled over with laughter, clutching her stomach. "Reed!" she gasped. "What was in your briefcase? I heard all that stuff hit the ground. It was hilarious!"

Reed's face fell. "Hilarious?"

"Yes," Piper said, trying to put on a straight face. "But in a good way." Then she exploded with laughter again. "Can I have a pencil and some pins?"

Reed puffed himself up to his full

height. "You laugh now, but the election is in one week, and from the looks of it, I'm the only candidate who's prepared to greet the public."

Jeremy looked at Piper and shrugged. "The guy's got a point. He's light-years ahead of me."

"You did all right," Piper said with a coy smile. "Even without the buttons."

"Thanks," Jeremy said, flipping his hair off his forehead. "I appreciate that."

Madison looked from Piper to Jeremy, and back again. Could it be possible? Was her best friend flirting with her worst enemy? It certainly looked that way. Madison did not like it one bit.

"Piper, let's go," Madison said, tugging on her friend's bright green raincoat and pulling her away from Jeremy. "I don't need to remind you that we've got a lot to do today."

"Like what?" Piper asked, squirming to escape Madison's grip.

"Homework, the newspaper, the campaign posters," Madison said, ticking the activities off as she pulled Piper toward the front door.

Reed, who had been struggling to re-snap the locks on his briefcase, suddenly noticed that Madison was leaving. "Hey, Madison, I thought we had a date," he called. "Remember? Breakfast for two."

Madison pointed to Jeremy. "Take him," she said, then she ran out the front door.

Once the girls were out on the sidewalk, Madison put her hands on her hips and confronted her friend. "What's up with Jeremy and you? One second you're calling him a jerk, and the next you're falling all over him."

"Whoa!" Piper slammed to a halt. "What are you talking about? That is so random."

Madison narrowed her eyes at her friend. "I'm talking about you competing for the flirt-of-the-year award back at the radio station."

"I may have flirted"—Piper leaned forward until her nose practically touched Madison's—"but Jeremy started it." Then she turned and danced off toward the parking lot at Jitters, where she'd parked her bright yellow MINI Cooper.

"All Jeremy did was talk to you!" Madison shouted as she hurried to catch up. "You were the one drooling."

"Well, of course I was drooling," Piper said as she unlocked her door and hopped into the driver's seat. "I had to get up at the shriek of dawn, drive to your house, chug one cup of coffee, and wait around while you got to be interviewed. I'm still drooling!"

Madison slid into the passenger seat and fastened her seat belt. "It just looked like you and Jeremy had something going there."

Piper turned her car key, and the engine roared to life. "What do you care? You hate the guy."

This was true. Madison slumped down in her seat. Why would it bother her? "Sorry, Piper," she said with a sigh. "I didn't get enough sleep last night. I may be delirious."

"That's okay." Piper patted her on the knee. "Buy me a vente latte at Starbucks and I'll forgive you."

Two lattes later, plus a couple of crumpets with gooseberry jam at the Pike Place Market, Madison went home. She was back in her room by nine A.M.

The first thing she did was check her e-mail. Nothing again! Now she was really starting to get paranoid. What if he hated her letter? What if something had happened to him? Madison couldn't stand the waiting. She sat down at her desk and typed another letter.

> Dear Blue,
> Where are you?
>   Pinky

7

"Are you still here?" Madison's dad asked as he shuffled into the kitchen late Sunday morning in his terry cloth bathrobe. He went straight to the coffee-maker and poured himself a steaming mug of coffee.

Madison looked up from her seat at the kitchen table. She'd been doodling on the border of the *Seattle Times*. "Am I still here? That's a funny way to say 'good morning.'"

"No, seriously, all day yesterday you hung around the house," her father said, adding a dash of half-and-half to his cup. "And now again today. Something must be up."

Madison had to admit it was strange for

her to spend an entire day at home. But that's what she had done all day Saturday after the radio interview. Normally she would have raced off to meet friends at the Northgate Mall for a few hours of shopping. Or she might have hit the library and gotten a head start on a term paper. Then she would have gone for a jog around the Queen Anne Hill cemetery, done homework with friends, and afterward, caught a movie downtown. Instead, she stayed inside the house. All day. Waiting.

Madison had watched the Saturday-morning cartoons, then checked her e-mail. Next she cleaned her room, then checked her e-mail. She put in some seat time with her Environmental Science textbook, answering all of the study questions at the end of the chapter, not just the assigned ones. Then she checked her e-mail. After taking their golden retriever, Lily, on the shortest evening walk ever, she checked her e-mail again. She watched an old black-and-white movie on AMC, then checked her e-mail again.

Now, on Sunday morning, Madison was feeling restless and anxious.

"Nothing's up, Dad," Madison said, trying to sound sincere as she slipped a slice of bread into the toaster. "I just feel like staying home, that's all."

Her father rubbed the stubble of beard darkening his chin and stared at his daughter. He took another sip of coffee and mumbled, "You need to get out. Get some fresh air. Do something."

Madison's father was right. She'd been cooped up in the house for way too long. She needed to get out and have fun—and she knew the one person to call who could guarantee that.

"Alex!" Madison waved at the tall, lanky redhead as she stepped off the streetcar at the Pike Street station. It had only been half an hour since she'd called him and told him to meet her at the waterfront, but he was already waiting for her outside the Aquarium across the street. Alex was wearing a multicolored stocking cap and a long green scarf. He took off his cap and did a giant arm wave with it as if to signal her from far away.

"Come on, Maddy girl, time's a-wastin'," he called in a mock hillbilly accent. "There's fun to be had, and we're a-goin' to have it."

Madison skipped across the street to join him. "I'm so glad you were free today. I was going stir crazy."

"Anything for the future president of EHS," he said, taking off his cap and holding it to his heart. "Now, where would you like to go?"

Seattle's waterfront had a row of piers packed with restaurants, shops, food vendors, and street performers. They were already at the Aquarium, which Madison loved. And to the south were the ferry boat terminals. Madison wasn't sure which way to go first. "I've got an idea," she said. "We'll each pick an activity and surprise the other one."

"Me first." Alex grabbed her hand and dragged her away from the Aquarium entrance toward the next pier down the street.

"Where are we going?" she asked, stumbling to keep up with him.

"Where the painted ponies go up and down," Alex said, wiggling his eyebrows as he gave her the big clue. A burst of calliope music sounded from inside the glassed-in building on Pier 57 as a family of four came out the front doors. The mom, dad, and kids all had hot pretzels covered with mustard in their hands.

Madison clapped her hands. "The old carousel! Oh, Alex, I haven't been here since I was ten."

They went inside, and Alex bought two red tickets and handed her one. "Now usually you're supposed to eat a foot-long hot dog with a big order of fries, followed by some icky sticky pink cotton candy before you get on this beast-mobile," he explained as they waited in line to get on the merry-go-round. "It guarantees a better chance of barfing when you get off. But we'll skip the chow for now and just ride."

Madison picked a swan with a saddle, and Alex chose a tiger. As the carousel began to turn, Alex warned sternly, "Buckle up! This could be one rough ride."

For the next few minutes they spun round and round. Alex kept her in stitches as he rode his tiger backward or hanging off the sides. The funniest was when he put his feet down on either side of the tiger and stood up. He was so tall that the carved tiger went up and down on its pole without touching him.

As the carousel began to slow down, Madison thought how ridiculous she'd been, waiting for somebody she didn't even know to send her a letter. Friends she knew were much better.

Once they were off the carousel, Madison took Alex's scarf and tied it around his eyes. "My turn."

"Help! I'm blind!" Alex yelped as he sawed wildly with his arms in front of him. "I could fall off the pier and drown."

Madison took his hand and pulled him back onto the street. "Don't be such a baby and follow me. I've got a great surprise for you."

Before she'd left the house, Madison had looked up the address for Ye Olde Curiosity Shop, and that's where she headed now.

"I heard this place is amazingly bizarre," she explained as she led Alex down the waterfront. "It's got everything gross that you can imagine."

Alex lifted the edge of his scarf with his hand and peeked out with one eye. "You're not talking about Ye Olde Curiosity Shop, are you? My favorite place on the planet?"

Madison blinked in surprise. "I didn't know you even knew about that place."

Alex raised the scarf so it was tied like a headband around his forehead. "There's a lot you don't know about me, Missy."

"Okay, smarty-pants. Then you get to show *me* around." Madison gestured to the archway made of Northwest Indian totem poles that framed the entrance to the shop. "I'll just follow."

From the street, the shop looked like any other souvenir shop, its windows filled with giant conch shells, sand dollars, puka shell necklaces, and souvenirs. Inside, it had everything from shell-covered jewelry boxes and flower leis to hula skirts and glass floats from Japanese fishing nets. Madison and Alex wove their way through the narrow aisles to the "museum" at the back of the shop.

Madison couldn't help it. She kept looking over her shoulder to see if anyone resembling her dream version of "Blue" could be wandering the aisles at the same time.

Alex led her to a glass case and pointed

to a little black magnifying eyepiece. "Take a look at that couple," he said.

Madison squinted one eye shut and peered at the little bride and groom inside the case. "I can't believe it," she gasped. "They really are fleas."

Sylvester the old prospector looked more like petrified wood than skin and bone. But he didn't look gory at all, just dried up. It was the shrunken heads that totally grossed out Madison. "Are these real?" she choked, looking at the tiny puckered faces with tufts of black hair on top.

"Look at the eyelashes," Alex said, pointing to the shriveled closed eyes. "I think they're real." He glanced at the handwritten sign beside the display. "Yup. Made by the Jivaro Indians of South America."

Madison did an all-over body shiver and turned away. "I think I've seen enough of this place."

"All right, your wimpness, we can leave." Alex looped his arm through hers. "Where to now? Seattle's underground tunnels?"

Madison's knees locked. This was too much of a coincidence—Alex knowing all about the Curiosity Shop and now him mentioning the underground tours. Could Alex be Blue, her Heart-2-Heart pal? It would make sense. He was sweet, smart, and probably the funniest person she knew. Madison looked at her friend with new eyes.

"What's the matter?" Alex asked. "You look like you've seen a ghost."

Madison blinked several times. "Not a ghost, but I may have solved a mystery." Madison didn't know whether to mention the Heart-2-Heart program and find out that instant, or wait.

Alex ducked down, looking in her eyes. "You sure look strange. Are you positive you're okay?"

"I'm totally fine," she said, shaking her head. "I think I'm having a blood-sugar dip. What I need is ice cream."

"But, of course," Alex declared in a French accent. "Zat is ze cure for every zing."

They decided to head back to Queen Anne Hill and their favorite ice-cream shop, Coneheads. It was worth it. Madison ordered her favorite, Cookie Dough. Then she watched carefully to see what Alex ordered.

He chose Chocolate Chip Mint, not Cherry Garcia. But that didn't prove anything, because Coneheads didn't carry Ben & Jerry flavors.

They decided to eat their ice cream outside, even though it was a damp, chilly afternoon. For years they'd walked the streets around their school on Sundays on the off chance they might run into a friend.

They did bump into someone, but it wasn't someone Madison would exactly call a friend. Jeremy Drum, accompanied by a golden retriever, rounded the corner at Roy Street and headed straight for them. Jeremy was wearing a leather jacket and stocking cap pulled down over his ears, and Madison almost didn't recognize him. But when he lifted his head and caught sight of Madison and Alex, he seemed as shocked as they were to see him.

Alex spoke first. "Hey there, Jeremy," he called. "Do you live around here?"

"My grandmother does," Jeremy answered stiffly. "I just came by to walk Ruby."

Madison took one look at the beautiful golden retriever, and her heart melted. She knelt beside the dog and ran her hand over its shiny fur. "She's beautiful. Aren't you, girl?"

Ruby replied by giving her a swift lick on the cheek. Madison chuckled and scratched the dog behind the ears.

"Ruby is a sweetie," she said, nuzzling her face in the dog's thick fur. "I have a golden a lot like her."

"Ruby's very cool." As Jeremy spoke, he avoided making eye contact with Madison and directed most of his conversation to Alex. "I have to come to my grandmother's to get my dog fix. My mom's allergic to fur of any kind—cats, rats, guinea pigs, you name it."

"How did you find that out?" Alex asked.

"We tried them all with the same results—hives," Jeremy replied. "Finally we settled on goldfish. Not exactly man's best friend."

Alex took a loud chomp of his ice-cream cone and mumbled, "Well, at least fish don't bite."

Madison held up the remains of her ice-cream cone and asked, "Can Ruby have this cone?"

The golden retriever answered Madison's

question herself by wagging her tail extra hard.

"Sure," Jeremy said, still keeping his distance. "Ruby loves ice cream. Ben & Jerry's is her favorite."

"She's got good taste," Madison said as she offered her cone to Ruby, who inhaled it in one bite. "It's my favorite, too. Today you'll have to settle for Haagen-Dazs."

It was weird chatting with Jeremy. He actually seemed nice. It was hard to imagine him as the ogre she'd made him out to be in her story at Giorgio's pizza parlor.

Alex finished his cone and wiped the crumbs off his hands. "Now that the election campaign is launched and under way, got any surprises for us, Jeremy?"

Jeremy shot Alex a sly smile. "That's for me to know, and you to find out."

Speaking of the election sent little butterflies dancing in Madison's stomach. She hadn't given it a thought all day. She also hadn't purchased any art supplies or made a single poster. The vote was just one week away, and she hadn't even come up with a campaign slogan.

"Alex, you had to bring that up." Madison gave the dog a quick hug and reluctantly stood up. "That means the fun is over, and we have to get down to business."

"Hey, if it's not fun, don't do it," Jeremy said, looking directly at her for the first time. His steady gaze set her butterflies dancing even faster.

There was an awkward silence as the three of them stood in a circle around the dog, nodding. Finally Jeremy tugged on the dog's leash and turned to leave. "I'd better return Ruby to Gram, or she'll think she's been dog-napped. I'll catch you guys at school."

"Right." Madison waved good-bye. She and Alex stood on the sidewalk watching Jeremy round the corner and disappear behind a row of elm trees.

"He doesn't seem so bad," Madison said, continuing to stare in the direction where he'd turned.

"I used to like him," Alex said. "Until the Homecoming incident."

Madison sighed. A lot of things had changed because of that one embarrassing moment. Maybe that was behind her. After two and a half years she had finally had a quasi-normal conversation with Jeremy. Maybe they could all move on.

That night after dinner, Madison spent an hour with her family around the dining table, trying to brainstorm slogans for the campaign. Mr. and Mrs. McKay both used yellow pads and number-two pencils to make their notes. Even her brother, Sean, had a notepad. The whole family had glasses of water in front of them to keep themselves hydrated. They looked like the poster family for overachievers. Madison shook her head and thought, *No wonder I feel pressured to succeed.*

They consulted magazine and television ads for inspiration but were only able to come up with a few ideas for slogans.

All of her mom's slogans rhymed: "Hooray for McKay!"; "McKay Saves the Day!"; "Make Your Day with McKay."

The commercial-inspired slogans came from her father: "Madison Is the Real Thing"; or, "Like a Good Neighbor, Madison Is There."

Then there were her brother's feeble

attempts at hipness: "Madison Rocks!"; "Madison Is Da Bomb!"

None of it was very inspired. Madison began to wish she had a different name.

"It's not the name that wins elections, but the ideas," her father reminded her. "Do you have good ideas?"

Madison went to her bedroom that night wondering about her ideas and how best to express them to the Evergreen student body. She was so preoccupied with the election that she almost forgot to check her e-mail. Just as she was about to drift off to sleep, she checked.

Dear Pinky,

I'm here. Previous commitments drew me away from the computer for a few days, but I'm back. I'd ask you what you did with your weekend, but that might reveal your identity. I'd tell you what I did this weekend, but it would definitely reveal mine. I did think about you a lot, imagining us on our date at the waterfront and taking the underground tour. Then I imagined us sailing on Lake Washington. After that, we flew kites at Gasworks Park. Which always sounds like a good idea, but once the kite is in the air, what are you supposed to do—roll the string out and then roll it in? Is there something more to kite flying that I don't know about? We of course discussed our favorite books—mine being Go, Dog, Go! And yours, HORTON HEARS A WHO. After that, you advised me to "straighten up. Let the world know you care." And I told you to "loosen up. Let the world know you don't care." Then, just as we were about to kiss good night—I woke up.

Good night, Pinky, see you in my dreams!

Blue

8

Honk! Honk!
Madison threw open her bedroom window on Monday morning and looked down at the bright yellow MINI parked in her driveway. "You're early, Piper!" she shouted. "I'll be down in a minute!"

Madison had printed out her letter from Blue and she read it through for the twentieth time before carefully folding and tucking it into her purse. It was possibly the most romantic letter she'd ever read. Not that she'd read that many love letters. There was one from Roy Bograd, who'd sat behind her in third grade. But it was short and to the point: *I like u. Do you lik me? Roy*
Honk! Honk!

"I'm coming!" Madison yelled, checking her image in the mirror one last time. Blue had suggested she loosen up, and that's just what she had done. No more prim school-girl. Today Madison wore a black tank top and extra-tight torn jeans. She piled on cut-glass and beaded bracelets on one arm and then hung several long strands of beads around her neck. Instead of her Mary Janes, she wore her brother's black Doc Martens boots. Definitely a different girl.

Piper squealed when Madison came trip-ping down the front steps. "Nobody told me it was dress-up day today! Is it Sixties Day, or what?"

The administration at Evergreen High would often announce dress-up days like: Nerd Day, or 70s Day, or Back to the 50s Day. Piper loved those occasions and would spend hours shopping for her outfits. "Do I have time to go home and change?"

"Piper, relax," Madison ordered as she threw open the door to the little car and hopped inside. "It's not dress-up day."

"Then why do you look like that?" Piper asked, clutching the wheel of her car but not moving.

"I felt like it," Madison said with a shrug. "I was looking through my jewelry box, saw all these necklaces and bracelets, and thought it would be fun to wear them. They didn't go with my regular clothes, so I wore these. What do you think?"

Piper adjusted her horn-rimmed glasses and tried to speak in a calm voice. "What do I think? I think you are seriously losing it. Madison, kids want you to be the leader type."

"What does a leader type wear, business suits?"

Piper put the car in gear and lurched forward down the hill toward school.

"Of course not," she said. "A leader is a leader in fashion, not a follower of fads. What you've got on falls somewhere between hippie and skater girl. Is that the image you want to project?"

Madison ran her hands through her hair in frustration. "Maybe. Maybe the message I want to send is, 'What I wear is not who I am.' How about that?"

Piper cocked her head, seriously considering it. "You may have something, but let's run it by our committee first to see what they think."

Madison slumped down in her seat as Piper guided the MINI down the tree-lined streets of Queen Anne Hill toward Evergreen High. Since when did she need to consult a committee about her fashion choices? Piper was acting like Madison had done something extreme, like shave her head.

"This is a little ridiculous, especially coming from you, Piper," Madison said as they waited in the long line of cars turning in to the Evergreen High parking lot. "All I've got on is jeans, a tank top, and a couple of necklaces. It's no big deal."

Piper wasn't listening. She was distracted by the music blasting from a bank of speakers that had been set up at one end of the parking lot. It wasn't really dance music but more like marching music. Drums. She slowed, and rolled down the window. The sound was deafening.

All around them students were weaving through the parked cars toward the campus, rocking out to the rhythm of the drums. Other groups had clustered on the lawn in front of the old brick building and were dancing and clapping their hands in time with the music.

As Piper pulled into an empty parking space, Alex's gangly shape appeared in front of them. He hurried up to Piper's window. "We've got a problem. A very big problem."

Madison leaned across Piper and asked, "What is it?"

"I can't explain it," Alex said. "You've got to see for yourself. Liz Struthers and Lou Garcia called me when they arrived this morning. I rushed right over."

Madison got out of the car, worried that something terrible had happened to the school or, worse, to the people inside. She looked around. There weren't any ambulances or police cars. Besides, if something terrible had happened, why were all the students laughing and clapping? She hurried to catch up with Alex, who led them up the front steps two at a time, and into the foyer by the attendance desk.

"What is it? What's wrong?" she asked, looking for signs of vandalism or hurt people.

"Don't you see?" Alex pointed to the floor. Decals of footprints led the way to pillars and doors that were covered with cardboard cutouts of drums. Printed on the drums were the words THE DRUM BEATS FOR YOU!

As they followed the steps, it was hard not to march in time with the drum music coming from the parking lot. Every other drum had Jeremy's picture on it. In the main hall, a banner had been hung that read, MARCH TO THE BEAT OF A DIFFERENT DRUMMER!

In the atrium, which was at the center of the school, students were gathered around two guys with dreads playing congas in a ska rhythm while another chanted, "Got the beat, feel the heat. Drum's the man, let's repeat." Groups of kids were standing around the drummers, clutching their books and singing along as they rocked to the rhythm.

Liz Struthers raced up to join them, followed by Lou Garcia. "Thank God you're here," she said. "This is a disaster."

Madison pulled her group to the far side of the atrium. "Would everyone just calm down? Okay, it's clear that Jeremy Drum has pulled off a great launch to his campaign. But it's not a disaster. Frankly, it's pretty cool."

Alex grabbed Madison by the shoulders. "What's up with you, Maddy? Are you losing your competitive edge? And what's with the outfit? Is this Dress-up Day? I didn't realize it was Dress-up Day."

"No, it's not Dress-up Day!" Madison shouted a little louder than she meant to, but her friends were starting to make her crazy. "Just because I wear a different outfit, people think I'm in a costume."

Liz put her hand on Madison's arm. "Now calm down." She turned to the others and said, "I see what Madison is up to. She's going with the 'I'm just people' look. Clever. If Jeremy goes with 'I'm different, so join me' pitch, then Madison can counter with the 'I'm one of you' angle."

Madison squinted one eye shut. "But isn't that sort of the same thing?"

Liz rolled her eyes. "I don't know. You're the one in the 'Beads R Us' outfit. You tell me."

"Ouch!" Piper winced. "Over the top."

"Look who's over the top," Liz replied, pointing to Madison's torn knees and thick-soled shoes.

"Look, this election is *not* about clothes," Lou cut in, "so why don't you two just chill?"

Piper and Liz turned on Lou in a fury. Suddenly Madison put two fingers to her lips and whistled hard.

That startled everyone; they turned to Madison. She took a deep breath and said, "I think I know what's happening here. Jeremy *did* beat us to the punch. He did come up with a really clever campaign and we're in shock because this is the kind of thing we should have thought of first. Well, this election ain't over, folks—it's just begun. And Jeremy just issued us a challenge. I say we can meet it and beat it. What do you say!"

Alex nodded intently. "We're going for it."

"This is the group to win the election," Piper declared. "We need to get serious and get clever."

"Lunchtime rally," Liz said, turning to Madison. "You name the place."

"How about the Two Dot Diner?" Madison suggested.

Everyone nodded.

Just then there was a rumble of angry voices behind them in the atrium. Reed Rawlings and his campaign manager, Biff

Jorgenson, were having an intense discussion near Jeremy's drummers. From the gestures Reed was making, it looked like he was telling Biff that he needed to top this.

Madison grinned. "Looks like I'm not the only candidate who was caught sleeping this morning. Reed's also getting a wake-up call."

The first bell rang, warning them they had five minutes to get to first period. All of them raced off to get to their lockers before class. The vice principal, Ms. Hernandez, had put a stop to the drumming in the atrium, but the recorded music still blasted from the parking lot. It was fun watching the two lanes of students dance their way into the first-period classrooms.

Since it was Monday, Madison's first period was Advisory Group, which had gone from being her least favorite class to her favorite overnight. She didn't want to lose a second of time writing her Heart-2-Heart partner. She dove for the first computer she could find and logged on.

Mr. Wheeler, who had watched her run in, said, "Well, you're very different today."

Madison waited for Mr. Wheeler to ask her if today was Dress-up Day. Luckily he didn't, so she murmured, "My Heart-2-Heart partner suggested I shake things up a little, so I wore this. What do you think?"

"You and your partner are exchanging fashion tips?" Mr. Wheeler asked as he walked over to her computer station.

"Far from it," Madison said. "We're reviewing life choices."

"Interesting." Mr. Wheeler nodded his approval. "The program seems to be really working. Already three students from my Tuesday-Thursday group have said their Heart-2-Heart partners have helped them deal with some major problems at school and even at home."

"That's very cool," Madison replied. She wasn't surprised. Heart-2-Heart had certainly changed her life. She'd turned into a mushy romantic. And she loved it. Of course, she'd never tell Mr. Wheeler that.

Her teacher stood for a second staring down at Madison's blank screen before he realized she was waiting for him to move on. "Whoops. Sorry." He moved back quickly to his desk at the front of the room. "Carry on."

Madison chuckled. She'd already begun her letter.

Blue,

Your letter was worth waiting for. Our date sounded great. I particularly like rolling out the string and rolling it back in on the kite, which reminds me a lot of fishing. I guess there's a pay-off if you catch a fish after standing there for hours holding a rod with a piece of string and hook attached to one end, but if you don't, it feels a little like a waste of time. So on our next date, let's skip fishing and kite flying, okay? Maybe we can skate around Green Lake Park, or just ride the monorail back and forth from the Seattle Center down to Westlake Center Mall. And speaking of the Seattle Center, did you know I've lived in Seattle my entire life and have never been to the top of the Space Needle? It may have something to do with my secret fear of elevators. I'm always afraid the cable's going to snap. Do you think if you jumped up just before the elevator hit the ground, you'd be okay?

Confession: I took your advice and tried to "care less" and I actually had fun. Instead of agonizing over the perfect outfit to wear to make sure I kept up my perfect image, I totally went the opposite way. My friends are a little shocked—over clothes, can you believe it? But

I'm having a blast. Maybe I really will dye my
hair pink. Thanks for the advice.
                                    Pinky, the Wild Child

Madison sent her e-mail and sat for a
full minute just smiling at her computer
screen. She truly felt happy. Could this be
love? Ridiculous. She'd never even met the
guy. Then why did she feel that "bubble-
licious" feeling that Piper always talked
about when she fell head over heels for
someone? Was it too weird that she herself
had never felt this way about a real person
but was now getting googly about a pen
pal?

Rather than overanalyze the whole thing,
Madison decided to go with the flow and see
what the future would bring. She knew the
odds were slim that Blue would get her letter and write back before first period ended,
so she decided to focus on the election for the
remaining minutes before the bell.

Madison slipped open her very organized
binder. There was a clearly labeled divider
for every event in her day, including after
school. The last divider was labeled, PRESI-

DENTIAL CAMPAIGN. It held a sheet of paper with a few of the ideas her family had given her the night before. But there was nothing that could remotely compete with Jeremy's drumbeat campaign.

As she studied her short list of ideas, Leonard Watkins, Evergreen's resident nerd, walked past her down the aisle. Robbie Leonis had stuck a note to Leonard's back *again.* This time the note read, DELETE. Several students snickered as he passed them, and Leonard instantly knew what was up. His expression didn't alter one iota as he felt his back, found the note, crumpled it without reading it, and tossed it into Mr. Wheeler's trashcan.

Madison was impressed by Leonard's cool reaction. But she was even more impressed with what she had just seen, and the idea that it had given her. She couldn't wait to tell the Elect Madison Committee about it at their emergency lunchtime meeting. She scribbled a few thoughts about her new idea into her notebook and zipped it into her pack.

She glanced up at the clock. Two minutes to go before the end of class. As she reached to switch off her computer, there was a *Ding!* letting her know that she'd gotten mail.

> Pinky,
> I made a few changes myself, and things are really starting to turn around, thanks to you. I certainly like writing you, but I can't help wondering what it would be like to talk to you. I'd like to hear your voice. Do you want to hear mine? If so, call me Wednesday night at 7 p.m. I'll be at this number—555-2934. We don't have to break our vow of anonymity.
>
> Woo-hoo! Blue
>
> P.S. I have to be away from my PC for a couple of days, so I won't be able to e-mail you until after we've talked.

Ring! The bell prompted a stampede for the door. Mr. Wheeler shouted over the din, "Computers off. If I find any on, you'll be docked a grade."

In her haste, Madison hit delete by accident. Her precious letter from Blue was gone! Rather than waste time trying to retrieve it and risk damaging her GPA, Madison repeated the phone number out loud to herself as she searched for something to write it on. "555-2934. 555-2934. Aaaah!"

Madison couldn't find a piece of paper. She'd already put her notebook away.

"Leonard!" She grabbed his sleeve as he shuffled back to his seat for his books. "Please give me something to write on."

Leonard paused for a second, as if he was wondering if she was planning to pull something on him. Finally he pulled a pad of Post-it notes out of his backpack and gave it to her. "You can keep it."

"Thanks, Leonard," Madison murmured as she hastily wrote Blue's number down. "You saved my life."

On an impulse, she gave Leonard a hug. He responded by hugging her back. For a brief moment, Piper's words ran through her head, warning her that Leonard might be her Heart-2-Heart pal. She pulled back and asked, "Do the words Pinky or Blue ring any kind of bell with you?"

Leonard frowned. "Are they some kind of rock group?"

"Hooray!" Madison hugged him again. He wasn't Blue! And, looking at Blue's phone number, Madison realized that Leonard had given her a great idea . . .

9

The lunchtime meeting was to take place at the Two Dot Diner, which was only three blocks from Evergreen High. As she cut across the parking lot, Madison was nearly mowed down by an ice blue BMW. Reed Rawlings was the madman behind the wheel. He screeched to a stop right in front of her.

"Reed, are you trying to kill the competition?" she shouted. "Is that your strategy?"

"Not a bad idea," Reed said, laughing as he rolled down his window. "Wish I'd thought of it."

Madison inched herself away from the front bumper of his Beemmer. "What do you need?"

Reed leaned his elbow on the open window and flipped up his Armani sunglasses. "I don't need a thing except an answer from you, darling."

Madison tried to hide her irritation. "I'd give you an answer if I knew the question." She forced a smile and added, "Honey."

"The question is, when do you and I meet for our breakfast rendezvous?" Reed caught hold of her hand. "This weekend?"

Madison winced. Did he really think she'd agreed to a breakfast date? She'd already told him no once. It was hard to avoid it again, especially since she *was* grateful that he'd arranged the radio interview.

"I don't know, this weekend's pretty tight for me," she hemmed and hawed. "I've got so many—"

"Excuses, I know," he finished for her. "Look, Madison, face facts. You and I are going to get together." He winked and added, "It's just a matter of time."

Reed slammed his car into reverse and zoomed backward through the parking lot. As he powered forward onto the street, Madison yelled, "Not if you drive like that!"

Madison raced to make up the lost time.

She was a girl with a mission. Just a block from the Two Dot Diner was Stampede Stamp and Art Supply. She ducked into the shop and quickly filled a basket with neon-colored pens, and some more pads of self-stick notes.

She was the first to arrive at the Two Dot Diner, a Seattle classic, with red leatherette chrome stools at the counter and a row of comfy booths. The food was fast, good, and cheap, which made the place a favorite hangout for Evergreen students. Madison slid into an empty booth in the back and set to work putting together her demonstration models. Then, as Piper, Alex, Liz, and the others trickled in, she slapped a sticker on each of their backs, like the one she'd seen on Leonard's back in Mr. Wheeler's class.

Alex read Piper's sticker out loud: "'Stick with Madison.'"

Piper read Alex's. "'I'm stuck on Maddy!'"

Liz, whose own sticker read, "'Winners Stick Together. Vote Madison,'" clapped her hands together. "Madison, you're brilliant. Everyone at Evergreen will go into sticker shock."

"Way to *stick* it to Jeremy Drum!" Piper

giggled, making a note of her pun on her yellow pad.

The others started tossing out their own sticker slogans. Mouse called out, "'I'm stuck like glue on you-know-who.'"

When the waitress came to take their orders, the group continued the joke.

"'I'm sticking with a hot chocolate and a bagel,'" Lou Garcia said.

When Alex asked him if he'd like a peppermint stick with that, the waitress responded, "'Stick with the menu,'" which made everyone burst out laughing.

By the time the group got back to school an hour later, they were armed and ready for their sticker attack. Lou Garcia and Henry Cooney positioned themselves near the gym. Alex and Piper took the front entrance, while Mouse stood at the ready by the stairs to the second floor. Liz and Madison roamed the Main Hall. Everyone they knew (and many they didn't) received a I'M STUCK LIKE GLUE ON YOU-KNOW-WHO! sticker on their back as they passed by on their way to class. Madison slapped STICK WITH MADISON notes on lockers and walls.

With only a minute to spare before the

start of afternoon classes, Madison's committee met to congratulate themselves on their "brilliant comeback," as Piper called it. Each agreed to go home and work up more stickers for the next day.

Then Piper and Madison hurried off together to their American History class. On the way into class, Madison remembered Blue's phone number. She searched her bag for the Post-it she'd written it on. She started to panic. It was gone!

She flattened herself against the wall outside the classroom so Mr. Dalberg wouldn't see her. "Omigod! Omigod!"

The bell rang. Piper ducked under the window of the door and hissed, "Madison, what's the matter with you?"

"I've lost it," Madison muttered. "The phone number. It was on one of those stickers we used."

"You can call information," Pepper whispered, crawling farther away from the door so the teacher wouldn't see her, either. "It's no big deal."

"Piper, you don't understand," Madison groaned. "It's Blue's number. I don't even know his name."

Piper rolled her eyes in frustration. It was clear she thought Madison was going way over the top over the loss of her Heart-2-Heart pal's number. But rather than lecture her, Piper just took a big breath and said calmly, "You know, you can just write him back and ask him to send it again."

Madison was on the floor, pulling everything out of her bag. "He said he's going to be away from his computer," she fretted. "On Wednesday he'll wait by the phone and I won't call, and he'll think I don't care. This is a disaster."

Piper frowned. "Madison, you are verging on becoming a complete Looney Tune. You don't even know this guy—"

"I do, too!" Madison interrupted. "I know how he thinks, what he feels, what he cares about. I just don't know what he looks like."

"Okay, okay!" Piper said. "I'm your friend, remember? I'll help you find the number. Do you remember the color of the pad?"

"No," Madison mumbled. "I was too excited to notice."

Piper shrugged. "Okay, the number's not

lost. It's just on one of the stickers we plastered everywhere. Now all we have to do is find it."

The girls looked at the long line of lockers extending down the hall. They were covered with dozens of Day-Glo I'M STUCK ON MADISON stickers that gleamed in the afternoon light.

"But it may take a while," Piper added.

Madison heard Mr. Dalberg's voice booming from inside the classroom. They'd have to be careful. Being caught cutting class was an unexcused absence, and it only took two of those to drop your grade a full point. "We have to be sneaky," Madison whispered. "Can't let Mr. Dalberg see us."

The two girls stashed their backpacks in Piper's locker and split up. Madison took the north end of the hallway, and Piper took the south. As she passed the main office, Madison tried to look like she was out on official business. She walked in long, purposeful strides toward the bank of lockers. But once she got to the lockers, it was hard to avoid looking like she was up to no good. One after another she flipped up the stickers on each locker, looking for the magic number.

Madison had covered one side of the hall without success, and was just bending down to check the first locker on the other side, when a familiar voice stopped her in her tracks.

"Looking for lunch money?" Jeremy asked.

Madison's face turned beet red. She slowly turned to look at Jeremy, who was standing with his hands in his pockets, watching her. "Of course not," she said. "Lunch is over."

"Then what are you looking for?" he asked, strolling toward her.

She folded her arms and stood her ground. "That's none of your business."

"Actually, it *is* my business," Jeremy replied. "That's my locker."

"What?" Madison spun to look at the locker. There was no way she could have known.

"Well, it's not what you think. I-I'm not planning on stealing from you," she stammered. "I'm just . . ." Her voice trailed off as she tried to think of a logical explanation for why she was standing alone in the hall with her hand on his locker.

Jeremy leaned his shoulder against his locker and grinned. He looked like the cat who had eaten the canary. "You're just what?"

Madison gulped and looked up at the I'M STUCK ON MADISON sticker on Jeremy's locker door. A lightbulb went on in her brain, and she tilted her chin in defiance. "I'm just removing this sticker from your locker." She reached up and tore the decal off the locker. As she did, she spotted the phone number on the back and screamed, "I found it!"

Jeremy jumped back two feet in alarm. "Could you shout a little louder?" he cracked. "I don't think the hall monitor heard you."

"So what are *you* doing lurking out here?" Madison asked, cradling the sticker with Blue's number in her hand, so Jeremy wouldn't see it.

Jeremy leaned in until his face was only inches from hers, and whispered, "That's for me to know and you to find out."

"Ahem!" a deep voice sounded behind them. "I hate to interrupt this little tête-à-tête, but don't you have someplace else you ought to be right now?"

Madison and Jeremy sprang away from each other like startled pigeons. They turned and guiltily faced the principal. Madison spoke first. "Hello, Mr. Kaufman. I left some, um, material for my report for Mr. Dalberg's class in my locker and I was just about to get it."

"Is that your locker?" Mr. Kaufman asked.

Jeremy cut in. "Actually, it's my locker. Madison forgot to mention that she had asked me to keep it for her." Jeremy spun the combination on the lock to show Mr. Kaufman that he was actually getting the report. He swung open the locker and grabbed the first thing he could put his hands on—a *MAD* magazine.

Without skipping a beat, Madison took it and started talking. "You see, Mr. Kaufman, we're studying the role that periodicals and newspapers have played in American historical events. For instance, um, Tom Paine's pamphlet *Common Sense* helped start the American Revolution, and, well, Horace Greeley's editorials in the *New York Tribune* sparked the great Westward migration and the idea of

Manifest Destiny, and now *MAD* magazine has, um, er—"

"Redefined the concept of social satire in the twentieth century," Jeremy jumped in. "Without *MAD,* there'd have been no *National Lampoon.* Without the *National Lampoon,* no *Saturday Night Live.* Without *SNL,* there'd be no Bill Murray. Eddie Murphy. Adam Sandler. The list goes on and on."

"Really?" Mr. Kaufman raised one eyebrow. "Very interesting."

Madison plastered a grateful smile on her face and extended her hand to Jeremy. "Thanks for keeping this, um, research material for me."

Jeremy shook her hand politely. "Anytime, Madison. I have room in here for lots more of your, uh, reports."

Before Mr. Kaufman could say anything, Jeremy shut his locker, and the two of them marched off in opposite directions away from the principal.

As she walked away, Madison held her breath waiting for Mr. Kaufman to call them back. But he didn't. Madison couldn't believe her luck. What a bizarre encounter!

And, yes, she had to admit it: Jeremy had really bailed her out when she'd run out of gas with her excuse.

By the time she got to the end of the hall, Madison had pushed all thoughts of Jeremy Drum and her close call with the principal out of her mind. She was focused totally on Blue, and the number in her hand. She could barely contain her excitement as she came around the corner into the South Hall.

Piper was methodically pulling up each sticker in the long line of lockers.

"I found it!" Madison squealed as she raced to join her friend. "I found Blue's number."

Piper grabbed Madison by the arm and pulled her into the janitor's closet under the stairs. She shut the door and pressed her ear against the door to make sure she didn't hear any footsteps coming down the hall. After a few seconds she turned to Madison with her hands on her hips. "You are insane," Piper fumed. "We have just blown off Mr. Dalberg's *extremely* difficult American History class so you could find the phone number of a guy who could turn out to be a total perv. On top of that, you are planning to call him, which, as I recall, is currently against the Heart-2-Heart rules."

Madison perched on the edge of the oversized industrial sink. "Look, Piper, I know I sound like a lunatic, but I really like this guy, and I'd like to talk to him. That's all it is. We're not even going to tell each other our names."

Piper flipped over a metal bucket and sat down. "Let me offer you some advice," she said. "First of all, be careful what you say when you two talk. This program works for a lot of people. Liz says she's really starting to open up. Unfortunately, I figured out who my Heart-2-Heart pal was on our second e-mail. All I needed were a few clues. He said *South Park* rocked, Bart Simpson was his hero, and he confessed that he had personally logged over a thousand hours playing "Halo" on his Xbox."

"Martin Robeler?" Madison guessed.

"Bingo." Piper touched her finger to her nose. "And do I want to date him? No. Do I even want to share another thought with him? Absolutely not. My Heart-2-Heart pal and I are through. End of story. Do you want that to happen to you?"

Madison knew what her friend was saying was probably true. Once she spoke to Blue, everything would change. But she secretly hoped it *would* change—for the better. Here she was, almost a senior, and she had never had a boyfriend. She had gone out on a few dates with friends, but never with someone who had made her heart skip a beat just thinking about him. And as over the edge as it sounded, Blue was doing that to her. She couldn't wait to talk to him!

10

Wednesday night. The moment she'd been waiting for was finally here.

Madison knew right away what she had to wear for this, the most important phone call of her life. Pink. She chose a pink cashmere sweater, and a pink silk skirt with a silver rose pattern. She'd even stopped by the drugstore on the way home and bought some "Pretty in Pink" lip gloss, just for luck. If her friends hadn't reacted so badly to her retro-punk torn jeans and black tank top she might have even thrown caution to the wind and dyed her hair, or at least the tips of it, pink. As a compromise, she bought a can of pink spray glitter and, again, just for luck, sprayed a soft mist of pink sparkles over her short dark hair. It was crazy—he couldn't even see her! But Madison knew it was for luck. Now, as seven o'clock approached, she found her heart fluttering wildly in her chest. Worst of all, she couldn't stop her hands from shaking.

The Post-it with Blue's number on the back was spread out neatly beside the phone. Madison really didn't need the little slip of paper anymore. She had chanted the number to herself over and over like a Buddhist mantra, until now those seven little digits—555-2934—were forever etched in her memory.

The minute hand moved forward one notch on her alarm clock.

"Seven o'clock," she told her reflection in the mirror. "Showtime."

Madison picked up the portable phone and started to dial, then quickly set the phone back down again. She didn't want to seem too anxious. She could at least wait a minute or two.

She applied another layer of pink lipstick over the other five layers already on her lips. Then she curled her mouth into a pout and said, in a sultry voice, "Hi there, I'm Pinky."

Nope. She didn't want to come off as too loose. She stuck a perky smile on her face. "Well, hello there! It's me!"

Whoa. Way off the cute-o-meter. Why not skip the hello completely?

"What's up?" Madison asked, in her most noncommittal voice.

No. *Too* noncommittal. She didn't want to sound like she didn't care. She was about to try another tack when she realized the minutes had ticked away. It was now 7:05. Better call. Quick.

Madison picked up the phone, tapped in the number, and waited.

One ring. Two. Three.

Madison watched her eyes widen in the mirror. What if this was another cruel joke played at her expense? She'd had enough of those.

On the fifth ring, a male voice answered. "Hello?" He sounded out of breath, as if he had run for the phone.

"Blue?" Madison asked. "Is that you?"

"Yeah, it's me," the warm voice responded. "We don't have a good connection—I'm on a cheap cordless. But I like your voice. Much better than a letter."

Two hours later, Madison and Blue were still talking. It was getting harder and harder to stay anonymous. She wanted to tell him everything: about the election, about the other candidates; she even was willing to tell him about the great Homecoming disaster—but all of it would have been a dead give-away.

Instead, they talked about their likes and dislikes. His favorite color was blue, and hers was purple, not pink. She admitted to being the kind of person who ate an Oreo bit by bit. First she took it apart and licked the frosting off, and only then did she eat the cookie sides. On the other hand, Blue liked the sandwich aspect of an Oreo and ate it all in three bites. They both thought riding the ferries to any island in Puget Sound was the best. Blue had actually flown in a hydroplane and landed in a bay in the San Juan Islands. Madison told him about her hydrofoil trip to Victoria, Canada.

They shared their hopes and dreams for the future.

"I've toyed with becoming an influential rock star, sort of like a Kurt Cobain without the suicide," Blue confessed. "But I have a feeling I might make a better forest ranger."

"I fantasize about becoming a famous author and living in a villa by the sea in Italy," Madison said. "But my dad thinks I should become a lawyer. He's probably right."

They both agreed on the five jobs they absolutely would never want to have.

"Those people who stand in toll booths in the rain must be miserable," Madison said. "And guys who write up parking tickets—people hate them."

"People also hate referees," Blue said. "I wouldn't want that job, either."

"How about really gross jobs?" Madison said.

"You mean like guys who pick up road-kill?" Blue asked.

"Ew!" Madison wrinkled her nose. "Like that."

"And the grossest job of all," Blue added. "Guys who work for those diaper services. They have to open those bags of dirty diapers and wash them."

"That wins!" Madison said, giggling hysterically.

Their conversation drifted all over the

map. They made sure to stay away from subjects like school and friends. But there was still so much to talk about.

"I'd like to go to Ireland someday," Madison said, lying on her back on her bed. "My family still has relatives there . . . out in Kerry, I think."

"I believe that is a clue," Blue pointed out.

Madison giggled and rolled over onto her stomach. "You're right. It's a big clue. Where would you like to go?"

"I'm leaning toward a jungle place, like the Yucatán in Mexico, or Belize. I've always wanted to climb one of those Mayan pyramids." Then Blue added, "But my family is not from there."

"Which is also a clue," Madison said.

"True," Blue said with a deep chuckle. "By process of elimination you can assume that I am probably not Lou Garcia."

Madison made a mental note. *He knows Lou well enough to use him as an example. Of course, everyone in school knows Lou. Aside from being a football player, he's just an all-around great guy.*

"Now that I know you are not Lou,"

Madison said coyly, "that leaves 1,199 students to choose from. Using the process of elimination, I should be able to subtract about a student a day. At that rate, I'll be able to discover your true identity in a little over three years."

"Aha!" Blue said. "Another clue. You are a mathematical whiz. And you know how many students there are in our school, so that means you either care a lot about Evergreen, or you just have a real head for numbers."

Madison bit her tongue. She didn't want to respond to either statement. It could give her away. Madison and Piper had been on the math team since ninth grade. As there were only twelve kids on the team, and just five were girls, it wouldn't take anyone long to figure out who she was.

The more they talked, the more Blue's voice seemed familiar to her. She was certain they must have spoken to each other before, but she just couldn't place when or where.

Blue had the same feeling. "I have to confess that I know your voice, which means we must know each other," he said. "This could be a good thing, or a really awkward thing."

"Why awkward?" Madison asked.

"Well, what if we don't like each other?" he asked.

"That's not possible," Madison said, tracing the tiny floral pattern on her duvet. "We have so much in common, and we totally agree on so many things. Even if we've met before, we probably don't *really* know each other."

"I believe that," Blue said. "There are so few people at our school who know what I think or feel. They all have their opinions about me, but they don't know *me*."

Madison felt the same. Piper, her best friend, knew her in one way. But there were so many other thoughts and feelings that she had never shared with Piper. "I suppose that's true of everyone," she said.

Bam! Bam! Bam!

The sound of her brother pounding on the door burst into their conversation like an explosion. Madison immediately sprang to her feet, fearful that her brother might call her by name and give away her identity.

"Hold on, Blue," she whispered. "My brother's at my door. I'd recognize his fist anywhere." Madison buried the phone under her pillow and went to open her door. "You pounded?" she said to Sean.

"Mom told me to tell you that she'd like to use the phone, Dad wants to use the phone, and I need to make a call," Sean bellowed in her face. "So you'd better get off the phone *now!*"

Madison slammed the door. She pulled the phone out from under her pillow and whispered, "Are you still there?"

"Of course."

"I'm sorry, but I have to go now," she said. "Apparently I'm not the only person in this house who wants to use the phone."

Blue chuckled. "Then I will say farewell."

"Forever?" Madison asked, in a sudden panic. "I mean, will we talk again?"

"You can count on it," Blue replied.

Madison hung up, but immediately dialed the number back. When he picked up, she said, "I forgot to tell you how much I liked talking to you this evening."

"I did, too," he replied. "I guess you could call it our first date."

"First?"

"Of many," Blue replied. "I hope."

"Me too."

They said good-bye again. Madison sank back in her bedcovers, cradling the phone to her chest. Everything about Blue was so romantic! She closed her eyes, trying to imagine the face that went with that wonderful, warm voice.

Her thoughts were interrupted by a *Ding!* from her computer. A letter! From Blue! She couldn't get to the keyboard fast enough.

> Dear Pinky,
> I love your letters, your voice, your mind. I'd like to see your face. Should we break the rules and meet in person? I think so. How about Friday at 4 p.m. at the Space Needle? I'll wear a blue carnation.
>
> Blue

Madison immediately keyed in her reply:

It's a date! I'll be wearing a pink rose.

11

"Maddy, catch!" Alex hurled a stack of papers wrapped with a rubber band across the layout table. "These need to be proofread and all changes inputted before eight A.M. Liz's orders."

"Where is Liz, anyway?" Maddy demanded, quickly flipping through her assignment. "She's the one who asked us to come in early, and she's the last to arrive."

"I heard that, McKay," Liz's voice boomed from the doorway. "And to answer your question, I've been running my tail off since six this morning." She dropped her black nylon Prada bag on the table and hung her charcoal gray wool coat on the standing rack by the Journalism room's door. "Biff Jorgenson didn't like the photo we were using of Reed, so he had me pick up the one they made for Reed's campaign."

"Reed wouldn't let one of our staff photographers come near him," Kirk Boyd, the assistant editor, called from his computer terminal across the room. "Said he wanted to have a professional do it."

Alex shook his head. "That must have cost mucho bucks."

Adjusting the big, black-framed glasses on his nose, Kirk peered at them above his monitor. "Apparently the guy's rolling in dough."

"How are we doing?" Liz said, draping her arm over Alex's shoulder and studying the proof of the new front page of the *Eagle's Cry* that was spread out on the table. She read the headline out loud: "'Election Countdown!' I like that. Now where's the center section?"

Alex flipped up his LIFE IS GOOD visor. "Ask Maddy. She's still working on her 'Vote for Me' statement."

Maddy winced. "It's done, Liz, I swear. All except the last sentence."

Liz crossed to Maddy's computer. "Call it up. Let me take a look."

As Maddy opened the file, Alex added, "Make her show you the article she wrote raving about the Heart-2-Heart program. I've got a big blank spot here on the front page just waiting for that piece."

"Alex! I e-mailed that to you fifteen minutes ago!" Maddy shouted, taking a swig of coffee and a quick bite of a rock-hard bagel. "Wake up."

"Victory!" Jake Lasko cried from the door. The paper's star reporter hurled his letter jacket onto a chair as he came into the Journalism room. "KYXX loved the radio interviews so much that they bought a half-page ad for the election issue. And Jitters said they'd spring for a quarter page."

"Way to go, Lasko!" Liz cheered. "But we'll have to go to warp speed to build the ads."

"I'm psyched for it," Jake said, leaping over the back of his chair and landing with his hands on the keyboard of his PC. "Let's rock!"

Fridays were always crazy in the Journalism room, but today seemed to be especially wild. The election campaign had pumped everyone into a frenzy. This issue of the newspaper was twice as thick as usual, and the *Eagle's Cry* staff had come in early to make their nine A.M. deadline.

Madison had another reason for being so pumped. Today was the day she would meet Blue! Their date was set for four P.M., and how Madison was going to survive the agonizingly long hours until then, she didn't know.

Padarrump! Padarrrump! The crisp beat of a snare drum in the parking lot signaled the arrival of Jeremy's supporters. Piper turned the handle on the window and pushed it open. The room was instantly filled with the big, loud *boom!* of a bass drum.

"Whoa! Check this out!" Piper shouted over her shoulder. "Jeremy's band is filled with every punk, Goth, and skater at Evergreen!"

The *Eagle's Cry* staff left their computers and ran to look out the window. Below them, the oddest collection of drummers was snaking its way along the low brick wall that lined the front sidewalk at Evergreen High. Some had real drums like bongos or congas, but others were beating trash cans with drumsticks or banging on pots with wooden spoons. They all followed Sierra Faith, who carried a large poster that read, JEREMY DRUM BEATS FOR YOU!

Alex gave Madison's hand a squeeze and whispered in her ear, "Don't let 'em scare you, Maddy. They're still the fringe."

Madison closed her eyes as Alex spoke. Had it been *his* warm voice she'd listened to last night on the phone? She couldn't tell.

Jake Lasko grabbed a camera with a massive telephoto lens from off their adviser's desk. "I gotta get a shot of this," he said, focusing the lens on the marchers below. "Look at all the hair colors—green, blue, pink, silver, rainbow. This would make a great cover shot!"

Liz was at his side in a flash. "Over my dead body, Lasko! Have you forgotten whose side you're on?"

Jake lowered the camera. "I thought we were a newspaper reporting the news. Isn't this news?"

Liz chewed nervously on her lower lip. "It's news, yes. But not front page, okay? What do you say, Madison?"

"Go for it, Lasko," Madison said, closing

the window. "Put it in the election foldout. We have to be fair."

"Even with Jeremy?" Piper asked.

Madison shrugged. "He seems like an okay guy. Maybe he's changed."

"I don't think so," a deep voice answered from behind them. Lou Garcia filled the doorway in his green and white letter jacket. "Have you seen Main Hall?"

Madison shook her head. "I came in the side door by the parking lot. That was the only door open when I got here this morning."

"Lou, let me through!" a voice squeaked.

Lou turned sideways, and Mouse burst into the room. She flipped back the hood of her Evergreen High sweatshirt and bent over to catch her breath. "Oh, Madison!" she gasped. "It's just awful . . . I ran . . . up the stairs . . . all the way." Her words came out in breathless spurts. "You won't believe . . . what's in Main Hall . . . poster size . . ."

Alex didn't wait for Mouse to explain. He bolted out of the room and raced for the stairs. Madison and Piper were right on his heels.

The hallways were just beginning to fill up with students arriving for school. The

Stafford twins stood in a tight huddle by the water fountain, whispering furiously with several members of the pep squad. The whispering stopped abruptly when Madison went by.

Madison didn't know what to expect as she turned the corner into Main Hall, but she knew it would be bad. And it was.

Life-size posters of photos taken of her at freshman Homecoming covered the walls. There was a shot of her running to the royal float, grinning and waving to a shocked crowd. One of her stepping onto the float to join the dismayed winners. Another shot caught her with her face in her hands, leaving the stadium. The captions under the pictures said things like WRONG WAY MCKAY, or NO WAY MCKAY.

The drums were still beating outside the front doors of Evergreen High, but inside, the silence was deafening. All of them seemed to be holding their breath, waiting to see Madison's reaction. She tried to be brave, but her lower lip was trembling. All she could do was clutch Piper's arm and blubber, "Why? Why is he doing this to me?"

Suddenly her knees went all wobbly, and she started to lose her balance. Lou and Alex were at her side instantly, supporting her by the arms. Then everyone began talking at once.

"Find Jeremy Drum!" Lou shouted over the din to two teammates from the football team who had just entered the hall. "That guy needs a pounding!"

Reed Rawlings appeared in front of Madison with one of the posters in his hands. He ripped it in two. "Madison, are you okay? I just alerted Mr. Kaufman. He's looking for Drum right now."

Reed's actions prompted everyone around Madison to start ripping the posters off the wall. But the damage had been done.

By lunchtime, every student at Evergreen had heard about Jeremy Drum and the awful posters. And if they were freshmen, sophomores, or new transfers to the school, they had to be told the entire story of Madison McKay's legendary humiliation. The Stafford twins were more than willing to do the honors.

That week's publication of the *Eagle's Cry* was delayed while Liz Struthers wrote a scathing editorial about dirty politics and how they had no place at Evergreen or in the world. Of course, Jake Lasko's photo of Jeremy Drum's conga line was cut from the edition. Liz wanted to eliminate Jeremy's picture and personal statement from the paper completely, but Kirk Boyd talked her out of it. He pointed out that no one had actually proved that it was Jeremy who had put up the posters. It was unfair to assume it was Jeremy just because he was the likeliest suspect.

"Well, who else could it be?" Liz asked later over a quick lunch in the cafeteria. "It couldn't be Reed—he was the first to tear down the posters."

Kirk picked up his burrito supreme and let the salsa drip onto his plate before he took a bite. "I'd just like to hear Jeremy's side of the story before he's convicted and hanged without a trial. Has anyone found him yet?"

Madison, who had been feeling numb since that morning, roused herself to answer. "He's supposedly on a field trip with Mr. Ruskin's Art History class."

"Has anyone verified that?" Liz asked as

she carefully peeled her orange. "Because that would give him an alibi."

"Not necessarily," Alex countered. "He could have put up the posters before the class left this morning."

"Or he could have put them up last night when the building was unlocked," Piper declared as she stole one of Liz's orange wedges off her plate and popped it into her mouth. "Wasn't the French Club dinner last night?"

Mouse finished off a bag of Chee•tos and licked the cheese off her fingers. "I wonder where he got the photos," she said. "Were they in the school archives?"

Jake Lasko shook his head firmly. "No way. Dave Sterling was staff photographer that year, and I was his assistant. He only got snaps of the queen and her court."

"Maybe Jeremy took them himself," Piper suggested.

"The angle's all wrong," Alex said. "Those shots were taken straight on from in front of the bleachers. Jeremy was down in the tunnel by the drinks counter, right?"

Madison nodded. "So was Reed."

Kirk chugged his carton of milk and set

it back on his lunch tray. "Maybe they're from the *Seattle Times.* They always cover Homecoming. You'd have to have some connections to get them, but maybe Jeremy does."

"One thing for certain," Liz said as she tossed her orange peel in the trash, "Jeremy's chances of winning now are zip."

Alex agreed. "Nobody wants a jerk for a president."

His remark jolted Madison out of her depressed stupor. "Jeremy *is* a jerk!" she declared, slamming her fist on the cafeteria table. "He hurt me two years ago and he's trying to do it again. Well, this time I won't let him get away with it!"

"That's our Maddy!" Alex crowed, giving her a two-handed high five. "She takes no prisoners!"

As the day wore on, Madison got angrier and angrier. She tried to concentrate in American Literature, but Jeremy's face kept appearing in her mind. She'd think of him at the radio station, giving his phony "Everybody counts" speech, and that would make her mad. Then she'd remember him walking his grandmother's dog and smiling that bogus smile, and *that* made her furious. And when she finally remembered him repeating his coy phrase "That's for me to know and you to find out!" she was ready to explode.

As she was walking back to her locker after class, Madison spotted the yellow school bus returning from the field trip to the art museum. It pulled to a stop in front of the school, and one by one Mr. Ruskin's students disembarked. They were laughing and slapping at one another as they came down the steps. Jeremy was doing damage control on a verbal fight between Stacey Merrill and her on-again boyfriend, James Roland, when Madison suddenly appeared between them.

"Jeremy Drum!"

She yelled so loudly that Stacey and James completely shut up.

"You bellowed?" Jeremy asked, stepping forward. The smile on his lips vanished as Madison hammered him with her words.

"You think you can win this election by dragging up something embarrassing that happened over two years ago!" she shouted. "Well, you can't. You humiliated me once. But you will never, *EVER* do it again. Do you hear me?"

Jeremy held up his arms. "I have no idea what you're talking about."

Madison jabbed her finger in the air to punctuate her words. "You are a liar and a phony!" She leaned forward until her nose was inches from his. "And that's for me to know and the whole world to find out!"

Before Jeremy could utter a word of protest, she spun on her heel and marched out to the parking lot.

Piper had seen Madison power out of the school building and raced to catch up with her. She witnessed the whole confrontation.

"Girl, you were awesome back there!" Piper cried, clapping her friend on the back. "Jeremy didn't know what hit him."

Madison just stood there, fuming.

"This calls for a celebration!" Piper looped her arm through Madison's and pulled her toward her car. "Come on, we'll pig out at the food court in the Seattle Center. I'll drive."

"Seattle Center!" The color drained from Madison's cheeks. "What time is it?"

Piper checked her TechnoMarine. "Three thirty. Why?"

"Date! I-I have a date, an important

date!" Madison stammered. "Rose. Need a pink rose. Change clothes. By four o'clock."

Piper took Madison firmly by the shoulders. "Madison? Speak English!"

"Oh, Piper!" Madison wailed. "I'm supposed to meet Blue at the Space Needle. And I'm scared. Please, oh please, come with me!"

For once, Piper—the girl who was always ready with a quip—was speechless. She adjusted her red-and-black-checked glasses, folded her arms across her chest, and stared at Madison. Finally she shook her head and said, "Madison Louise McKay, you amaze me! You actually want me to drive you to the Space Needle to meet some mystery man you have never met but have fallen head over heels in love with because of a few letters?"

Madison nodded. Then she asked in a tiny voice, "So will you?"

"Are you kidding?" Piper flung open her car door. "I wouldn't miss this for the world!"

12

Piper's yellow MINI zoomed up Queen Anne Avenue toward Madison's home at the top of the hill. As they drove, Madison told Piper how her relationship with Blue had grown from a Heart-2-Heart pen pal to a full-fledged date. Piper took the turn onto Highland Drive on two wheels and screeched to a halt in front of the McKays' rambling Victorian house. She checked her rearview mirror nervously as she turned off the engine. "I hope nobody noticed we broke every traffic law on the planet."

"If you didn't want to be noticed, Piper," Madison joked, "you shouldn't have bought a bright yellow car."

The two girls leaped out of the car and

bolted for the front porch. Taking the steps in big strides, they charged through the front door past Madison's mother, who was working in the study, and up the stairs to Madison's bedroom. Piper, as the official timekeeper, checked her TechnoMarine again. "Okay, you've got four and a half minutes to change into your gown, Cinderella. Then it will take us five more minutes to get to Petals flower shop to pick up a rose."

"No need for that," Madison cried as she peeled off her denim jacket and skirt and dove into her closet. "I already bought the rose. It's on my dressing table."

Two perfect pink roses sat waiting to be plucked out of a crystal bud vase.

"Why two?" Piper asked. "Do you want me to wear one?"

Madison stuck her head out of the closet. "No! I bought two in case one wilted."

Piper chuckled and shook her head. "Remember when you asked me if you're excessive? My answer now is, yes. No one else on earth would think of buying a backup."

Madison hurriedly pulled on the pink

silk skirt with the silver rose pattern that she had worn for the phone call. Then she pulled a pale pink camisole over her head. Layered over that, she buttoned an antique blouse she'd found the day before at Secondhand Rose, a vintage clothing shop in Greenwood. It was delicate and feminine, and just the right choice for her first meeting with Blue.

Her hands shook as she fumbled with the pearl buttons that ran all the way up the high lace collar. "Oh, Piper, I'm so nervous," Madison wailed as she slipped her feet into a pair of silver ballerina flats. "You're going to have to help me with the rose."

"I'm on the job!" Piper pulled a pair of scissors out of the leather cup on Madison's desk and clipped one of the rosebuds from its stem. "Here. I'll pin this in your hair."

Madison grabbed two clips from her vanity and hurried into the hall. "Come with me to the bathroom. I have to brush my teeth."

Piper stumbled behind Madison, struggling to pin the rose in her hair. "You're going to have to stand still for at least a second," she ordered.

Madison frantically brushed her teeth, used two breath strips and, just for good measure, brushed her teeth again. "How are we doing on time?"

Piper checked her watch. "You're not stopping to buy flowers, so that'll buy you two more minutes. But we may have trouble finding a place to park, which could make us late."

"We can't be late!" Madison stuffed her toothbrush back in its holder. "Come on. We have to run!"

She led Piper back down the stairs, past her mother, who watched them curiously from the door of the study, back across the porch, and down the steps to the car.

As they jumped into the yellow MINI, Mrs. McKay stepped onto the porch. "Madison, what in the world is going on?"

"Can't talk, Mom," Madison shouted out the car window. "I'll tell all later! Wish me luck!"

Mrs. McKay looked completely befuddled. As the MINI roared away from the curb, she waved vaguely. "Good luck!"

Piper drove back down the hill a bit more sanely. They headed toward the Seattle

Center, which was where the Space Needle was located. Madison patted the rose in her hair for the umpteenth time and looked up at the big silver spire that towered above them. "Blue is probably standing up there at this very minute. Oh, God, I hope this works out."

"Now listen, friend," Piper warned as she turned left onto Mercer, the one-way street that bordered the north side of the Seattle Center complex. "If this doesn't work out, there are other fish in the sea. I can name ten guys off the top of my head who would die to go out with you."

"A spot!" Madison screamed, pointing to the opposite side of the street. "There! Park there."

With a squeal of brakes and tires, Piper fishtailed across three lanes of traffic and whipped the little yellow car into the vacant spot. Madison was out of the car before Piper could turn off the engine.

"Time?" Madison asked as they zigzagged between the oncoming traffic to the other side of the street.

"Two minutes and counting," Piper reported. "This had better be worth it."

The girls entered the Seattle Center by an access lane near the opera house, then hurried down a long sidewalk past the International Fountain over to the center of the huge complex. They didn't go inside but hurried past, on through the Fun Forest Pavilion and its midway of carnival rides, straight for the ticket booth at the base of the Space Needle.

The Space Needle, along with the rest of the exhibition halls, sports arenas, museums, and theaters that made up the Seattle Center, had been built for the 1962 World's Fair. At the time, the Space Needle was the most ultramodern structure on Earth. The restaurant and observation deck looked like a flying saucer set on concrete pillars six hundred feet up in the air. To Madison it always reminded her of something out of the old cartoon series *The Jetsons*.

"Hang on a minute!" Madison cautioned as they drew closer to the soaring tower.

There was a crowd of people milling around the base of the Space Needle. Madison saw moms pushing strollers, some guys on bikes, lots of teenagers with skateboards, not to mention the line of people waiting to take the elevator up to the top.

"Do you see him?" Madison asked.

"See who?" Piper replied. "I don't know who we're looking for."

Madison rolled her eyes in frustration. "He's wearing a blue carnation in his lapel."

"We'll have to get closer to see that." Piper checked her watch once more. "Thirty seconds."

As they neared the crowd, Madison panicked. She ducked behind a concession stand and flattened herself against the wooden wall. "Oh, Piper, I'm afraid! I like to think of myself as the kind of person who doesn't care about superficial things like looks—but what if he really is Leonard Watkins? Or some other truly geeky person?"

Piper folded arms across her chest and smirked at her friend. "I warned you about this. But you wouldn't listen."

Madison shut her eyes and thought of that wonderful long phone call with Blue. "His voice was so familiar . . . and ever since then I've been trying to identify it. I've closed my eyes and listened to conversations in the halls at school, trying to place him. At one point I even thought he might be Alex."

Piper blinked in surprise. "Would that be so bad? You guys are good friends. They say that's how the best relationships begin."

Madison winced. "I know, but I guess I hoped deep in my heart that Blue would be this killingly handsome guy who would make me go weak in the knees every time I looked at him."

Piper shrugged. "Shallow, but understandable." She checked her watch. "You are now one minute late for your dream date."

Madison clutched Piper's shoulders with both hands. "Please. You go look and tell me what you see."

Piper peeked out from behind the shed and instantly ducked back again. "Whoa. He's there, all right," she whispered. "Blue carnation, and everything."

"And?" Madison searched her friend's face for some clue to her response.

"And he's waiting by the ticket booth for the elevator."

"That's not what I meant, and you know it!"

Piper cleared her throat. "Well, I've got good news and bad news. Your friend Blue is very attractive. I might even say he's that weak-in-the-knees kind of attractive."

"Really?" Madison clasped her hands to her chest in relief.

"He's also your worst enemy."

Piper pulled Madison around the edge of the shed to see for herself.

"Pinky? Meet Jeremy Drum."

13

Madison peeked around the concession booth and watched Jeremy Drum, his blue carnation pinned to the lapel of his black sport coat, search the face of every young girl who came by the Space Needle. He *was* handsome, weak-in-the-knees handsome, and his letters were wonderful. The phone call had been heaven. So how could such a handsome, wonderful person be so mean and rotten?

"Madison." Piper tugged on the sleeve of Madison's antique blouse. "It's been ten minutes. You can't just leave him hanging there. Even if he is a jerk."

"Maybe he isn't a jerk," Madison replied. "Maybe we've been all wrong about him."

Piper exhaled loudly. "Oh, come on. Homecoming? The posters? That's a jerk."

Madison chewed nervously on her already stubby fingernail. "Kirk said we've convicted him without a trial. Maybe I should give him a chance."

Piper shrugged. "It's up to you."

Madison made a snap decision. She took the rose out of her hair and handed it to Piper. Then she said, "Let me borrow your coat to cover all this pink I'm wearing."

Piper slipped her black-and-white-checked raincoat off her shoulders and put it on Madison. "Call me for backup if he starts swinging."

Madison threw her shoulders back and stepped out from behind the concession stand. She strolled casually toward the Space Needle. Jeremy was facing the other way, peering intently at the faces of two girls from Evergreen High who passed him on their way to the food court. She cupped her hands around her mouth and called, "Jeremy!"

Jeremy spun around, his face lit up with expectation. The second he spotted Madison, his shoulders slumped and the joy drained out of him. He glanced nervously over his shoulders and took a step toward her. "Look, if you've followed me here to lay another one of your insane diatribes on me, please don't. I've had about as much as I can take for one day."

"I didn't follow you," Madison protested. "And I'm not planning to say anything."

Jeremy kept on talking without really looking at her. He was too busy searching the crowd for a girl with a rose in her hair. "Let's just leave the battleground at school, okay?"

"I don't think of school or the election as a battleground," Madison replied, trying to defend herself.

"Yeah, right," Jeremy snorted. "Look, Madison," he said, putting his hands on his hips and finally facing her. "I don't want to be rude"—he paused for a second—"or maybe I do. But I have a date, and now is not a good time to talk."

Madison watched him push a lock of dark hair back from his pale blue eyes and thought, *Blue is a good name for him*. She tried to soften her approach. "So, is it anybody I know?"

Jeremy sighed impatiently. "I doubt it. She's not your type."

"Oh, really?" Madison said, feeling suddenly flirty. "What's she like?"

"This girl is beautiful on the inside and out." A warm smile played across his lips. "She's smart and funny. She's not so wrapped up in being cool that she's afraid to have a good time. And, above all, she's kind. She would never try to hurt anyone."

Madison was both flattered and confused. "So what is *my* type?"

Jeremy fixed her with an icy stare. "Your type is pompous, self-centered, and cruel."

His words hit her like a slap in the face. "Are you kidding?" she gasped.

"I'm deadly serious," Jeremy said, staring her down.

Madison was flabbergasted. "You're the one who's tried to humiliate me at every turn," she sputtered. "First at Homecoming, and now today at school. God, Jeremy, you define cruel."

"That's it!" Jeremy threw up his hands. "You and your vindictive friends have practically ruined my life. Why?" He pulled away

from her, visibly trying to calm himself
down. Finally he looked back at Madison.
"You have every right to run for president.
But you don't need to destroy me to do it.
Please, just leave me alone!"

Madison backed away from him, stunned.
His words were harsh enough, but the utter
contempt in his eyes was hard to take. No one
had ever looked at her like that before. She
stumbled back to the concession stand, where
Piper was waiting. "Let's get out of here."

As they were leaving, Madison grabbed
the rose out of Piper's hand and hurled it to
the ground.

The two girls rode home in silence. Piper
had witnessed the argument with Jeremy,
but Madison just couldn't bring herself to
repeat what he'd said to her. She was too
upset and completely confused.

When Piper dropped her off at her
house, Madison turned and said, "Thanks for
being there with me. You were right. It was
a big mistake."

Piper squeezed her hand. "I know you're
upset, so I'm going to keep my trap shut.
Call me later if you feel like talking."

Madison trudged up the porch steps and

in through her front door. Her mother called from the study, "So how'd it go? Were you lucky?"

Madison shrugged. "I guess." If "lucky" meant that she'd found out her "Dream Boy" was a nightmare, then she was very lucky.

She grabbed the banister and slowly made her way up the stairs to her room.

"Oh, Madison, you got a call from Reed," her mother called up after her. "He said he'll see you at six."

"Six?" Madison paused, trying to remember if she'd actually made arrangements to meet Reed. Impossible. She'd said no to breakfast. He'd suggested dinner, but she'd thought he was kidding.

Then again, she thought that might be the best thing for her to do. Go out with Reed. Forget about Blue and Jeremy, and maybe even have a *real* heart-to-heart with a real human being. Not a forced one like Mr. Wheeler's bogus program.

Madison climbed the stairs and changed out of her "Pinky" outfit. "I'm never wearing pink again," she muttered as she yanked off the pink skirt and antique blouse. She wasn't about to dress up for anyone anymore.

Madison slipped on a pair of jeans and pulled an olive green turtleneck sweater over her head. She wiped the pink lipstick off her lips and ran a brush through her hair. Then she slammed the brush down on her dressing table and faced the mirror. "There. It's the *real* me."

Twenty minutes later, as she was leaving her bedroom, the alert on her computer rang, signaling that she had mail. She guessed who it might be, and almost didn't check it. But curiosity got the better of her. She went to the monitor and clicked on the envelope.

Yep. It was from Blue.

Dear Pinky,
So there I was, wearing a blue carnation and a goofy smile. And there you weren't. I waited for an hour, then started to feel ridiculous. People thought I worked at the Space Needle and started asking me for directions. I would have thought I'd gotten the date or time wrong, but as I was leaving I

found a pink rose on the ground. Was it yours? The paranoid side of me thinks you might have seen me and were so turned off that you ran. The "There's got to be another reason" side of me says maybe you somehow didn't see me and so you left. So I'm writing this note in case you thought I'd stood you up, to let you know I was there . . . waiting.

Color me Blue

Madison read the letter over and over and felt awful. Maybe Jeremy was right: Maybe she *was* self-centered and cruel. She'd let him stand there waiting for her without a word of explanation.

For half a second, she thought she should respond, and make up an explanation that wouldn't hurt his feelings. But then a horn sounded outside.

Madison glanced at the clock on her bedside table. Six on the dot. It had to be Reed.

14

When Madison stepped out on her front porch, she found Reed leaning against the front fender of his silver blue BMW. He hadn't come to the front door to get her. It was clear he expected her to come to him. In his preppy cords and cable-knit sweater, Reed looked like he was posing for a magazine ad. His arms were folded casually across his chest, and he had one leg kicked back and resting against the wheel of his car.

Reed watched her through mirrored sunglasses as she came down the steps. Then he flipped open the passenger door. "I hope you're hungry," he said. "I made reservations for two at Windows on the Waterfront."

Madison paused at the door, confused.

"Reed, I didn't think we had a date. I made other plans, but they, um, were just cancelled."

"Excellent!" Reed said, helping her into the car. "That means we can spend the whole evening together."

Madison fastened her seat belt, trying to sort through what he'd just said. It sounded like they really didn't have a date. He'd just gone ahead and made reservations. Weird.

Reed hopped behind the wheel, slammed the gear into first, and squealed away from the curb. He flipped his sunglasses up on his head and grinned. "It's funny, I knew this would happen."

Madison blinked several times. "What would happen?"

He wobbled his thumb back and forth between them. "You and me finally getting together. It's destiny."

"What are you talking about?" Madison asked, with a frown. "We're just going to eat some food."

Reed power-shifted into second, then third. "I'm talking about freshman year when you shut me down."

Madison jerked her head back. "Huh?"

Reed chuckled to himself. "At first I thought you were playing hard to get. Giving me some lame excuse about going to Homecoming with your girlfriends."

Madison twisted in her seat to face Reed. "I *did* go with my friends."

"Yeah, right." He smirked, reaching for her hand. "You wanted me to beg you for a date."

Madison shook her hand away from him. "That is so *not* true," she said. "I wanted to be with the Float Committee because we'd had so much fun working together and we wanted to continue the fun. It had nothing to do with you."

"So did the fun continue?" Reed asked, raising an eyebrow.

"Of course not," Madison snapped. "You know what happened."

"*Tsk. Tsk. Tsk,*" Reed clucked, shaking his head. "You should have gone with me."

Warning bells were going off in Madison's head. She could tell this was going to be a disastrous evening. "Could you pull over?" she said suddenly. "We need to talk."

Reed kept driving, guiding the car off

Broad Street and onto Westlake Avenue North. "We're almost there."

"No, I mean it, Reed." Madison's voice was loud and firm. "Pull over now!"

"All right!" He swerved the car to the right side of the road, pulling up alongside Lake Union Park. "What's your problem?"

Madison forced herself to stay calm. "My problem is your warped perception of an event that happened two and a half years ago. It's way over the top."

"Hey! Who went over the top?" Reed snapped back. "You're the one who missed school for a week and then moped around the halls for months, just because of a harmless joke."

"*Harmless* joke?" Madison gasped.

"But that's all behind us," Reed said smoothly. He flashed a smile. "I'm interested in you and me—now."

"You and me?" Madison was getting goose bumps. Not the good kind, but the creepy ones.

Reed took her two hands in his. "Just imagine what the two of us could do if we combined forces."

Madison yanked her hands away from him. "I don't have a clue what you are talking about."

Reed flopped back against his seat in frustration. "The election," he said, as if the whole thing were obvious. "You and me— together. With our brains and looks, man, we could be one dynamic duo."

Madison tilted her head, trying to understand. "Let me get this straight. Are you suggesting that you and I run for office together?"

"Duh!" Reed said, with a wobble of his head. "With me as president and you as my VP, Drum wouldn't have a chance. Especially not after what happened today."

So much had happened during the day that for a second Madison thought Reed was referring to her heated exchange with Jeremy at the Space Needle. "But that shouldn't affect the election," she murmured.

Reed snapped his fingers in front of her face. "Madison, wake up! Those photos from the *Seattle Times* turned half of the school against him."

The warning bells she'd heard before turned into a full-fledged sirens. "How did you know those pictures were from the *Seattle Times?*" she asked, narrowing her eyes at him. "Most people thought they were from our files at the *Eagle.*"

Reed scoffed and waved one hand. "The *Eagle* doesn't have any shots of you from Homecoming," he said, as if he'd checked. "My mom said the guys at the *Times* keep archival photos of every major event at every high school in town."

Madison stared at him. "Your mom told you that," she repeated.

Reed shrugged. "Yeah. Sure."

Suddenly, things that had been fuzzy became crystal clear. Homecoming and the supposedly "harmless" joke. The poster-size photos that would make sure Jeremy lost the election. The suggestion that Reed team with her in the election bid for president.

Madison reached for the door handle and, keeping her voice as even as possible, said, "Reed, thank you so much for the dinner invitation and our little chat, but I just realized I have an apology to make. A very big apology. So I'll be leaving you now. Please, don't even think about following me."

Madison swung open the door and

hopped out before Reed could react. Then she started running. Away from the car. Back toward Queen Anne Hill.

As her feet pounded along the concrete pavement, she kept waiting to hear the sound of footsteps following her. But there were none. She remembered how Reed hadn't even bothered to walk up the stairs to ring her doorbell. He certainly wasn't going to run after her. No, he'd find some other way to get back at her. When she felt she was far enough away from Reed, Madison dug-in her bag for her cell phone and punched in the number that she now knew by heart.

"Five-five-five-two-nine-three-four," Madison murmured as she touched each number. The phone rang. And rang. No voice mail picked up. Finally, when Madison was just about to hang up, an elderly woman's voice answered. "Yes?"

"Hello, I'm looking for Jeremy Drum. Is this the right number?" Madison asked as she continued to walk back up the sidewalk toward Queen Anne Hill.

"Yes it is, but who's calling?"

"I'm Madison McKay, a friend from school."

"Jeremy is walking my dog right now," the woman said. "I'll tell him you called. If you'll leave your number—"

"No!" Madison shouted into the phone. She knew Jeremy would never in a million years call her back. "Don't tell him. I-I'd like to surprise him."

"Well . . . as I said, Jeremy's walking Ruby right now," she said. "He took her down to Lake Union Park."

Madison looked back the way she had come. She could see the park from where she was standing. "Oh, thank you!" she said. "I'll go try to catch him there."

Ten minutes later, Madison was circling the lake, looking for a tall boy with a golden retriever. As she ran, a plan began to form in her mind. She knew what she had to do.

She finally spotted Jeremy as he was walking the dog toward the park's exit. Madison was dripping with sweat and her hair was clinging in wet ringlets to her face when she caught up with them.

"Jeremy, wait!" she called, bending over to catch her breath.

When Jeremy saw her, he picked up his pace and hurried toward the crosswalk.

Madison threw her head back and moaned, "I can't keep up! Please stop."

At the intersection, he had to stop to wait for the traffic light, and she stumbled off the curb and stood in front of him, clutching her side.

"Please listen for one minute," she gasped. "I know that the Homecoming disaster wasn't your fault. I know you didn't put up those awful photos. And I am so ashamed for jumping to conclusions about you, and not ever giving you a chance to explain."

Jeremy opened his mouth to speak, and she held up her palm. "Just a minute. I'm not finished." She bent over once more and took a couple of deep breaths. "I know you'll never accept my apology because you think I'm heartless and self-centered. But just to prove to you that I'm sincere, I'm withdrawing from the race and throwing all my support behind you."

Madison waited for Jeremy to respond. As she looked into his eyes, he continued to say nothing.

She felt her throat tighten painfully. Tears pooled in her eyes. Madison turned to leave before she embarrassed herself any further. But as she stepped into the crosswalk, Jeremy caught her by the arm. "Now hold it a minute, will you?" he said, gently pulling her back onto the curb. "You just dropped an awful lot of information in my lap. The least you can do is give me a moment to process it."

Madison put a hand over her mouth, trying to hold herself together. Then she looked up into his pale blue eyes. They were no longer ice cold but filled with compassion.

"I guess I'll begin by accepting your apology," Jeremy said slowly. "And offer my own apology in return."

Madison laughed. "You apologize to me? Whatever for?"

"Excuse me," a man interrupted from behind them. He and a woman were walking with their tenspeeds. "This is a crosswalk. If you want to talk, there are plenty of places to do it over there." He pointed back to the park, by the lake.

They shared an embarrassed laugh. Then Jeremy led Ruby to a park bench and motioned for Madison to sit down. She perched on the edge of the bench, scratching Ruby behind the ears.

Jeremy pushed the hair out of his eyes and said, "I've relived that moment at Homecoming a zillion times. I felt so awful about pushing you onto the field, I didn't know what to do."

Madison asked the question she'd wanted to ask for two and a half long years. "Did you really think I'd won? Did you confuse McKenzie Madsen's name with mine?"

Jeremy shook his head. "I didn't even hear the announcement. I was holding Reed's place in the drinks line because he'd left to hear the announcement. When he came back, Reed told me you'd won. He ordered me to go tell you."

Madison slapped her hands on her legs. "I *knew* it! When Reed called it a harmless joke, I *knew* it had to be him. But why would he do that to me?"

Jeremy shrugged helplessly. "It turned out it really was just a joke. He had me tell you that so he could get your hot chocolates."

Madison's jaw dropped. "*That's* why he did it?"

"He was tired of standing in that long line." Jeremy kicked at the ground with the toe of his sneaker. "But I didn't know that at the time. When I pushed you onto the football field, Reed nearly fell over laughing. He thought he was so clever. I wanted to kill him!"

Madison shook her head in amazement. "Hot chocolate! He was willing to totally humiliate me for a couple of hot chocolates? I thought it was because I didn't go out with him."

"That also may have had something to do with it," Jeremy said, scratching his head. "He liked you, too."

"Too?" Madison repeated, cocking her head.

Jeremy flashed an embarrassed smile. "Well, at the time, I had a major crush on you. I thought it was pretty obvious."

Madison's heart skipped a tiny beat. Maybe all wasn't lost after all. "You did?"

He shoved his hands in his pockets and rocked back on his heels. "That's why I didn't apologize right away. I just couldn't face you. And later, when people like the Stafford twins and Piper Chang turned on me and started calling me names, I figured there was no way I could get anyone to

believe my side of the story. You and everyone else seemed to have made up your
minds."

Madison winced. "We convicted you
without a trial," she said, repeating the
words Kirk Boyd had said before.

Ruby chose that moment to lick Madison in the face, which made Madison burst
into giggles instead of tears. "It's funny how
things work out," she said, wrapping her
arms around the dog and squeezing her
tight. "All this time we spent hating each
other when we could have spent it—"

"Together." Jeremy kneeled beside the
dog and looked directly at Madison. "I guess
that's irony to the tenth power."

His mention of irony and math reminded
her that he not only was Jeremy, but he was
also her Heart-2-Heart pal, Blue. And only
two hours before, she had stood him up.
Madison didn't know how to bring it up. If
she confessed to being Pinky, would it look
like another conspiracy to make a fool out of
him? She couldn't decide.

Jeremy's face was inches from hers. She
could see little gold flecks in his eyes. Yes,
he definitely was weak-in-the-knees hand-

some. She managed to murmur, "I guess we're older now and, well, you have that girlfriend."

Jeremy's face reddened, and he looked down at his dog. "Um, I'm not so sure about that," he admitted, embarrassed. "I was supposed to meet her at the Space Needle today, but she never showed."

Madison's heart ached seeing him look so defeated. She wanted to blurt everything out right then, but something made her keep her secret. Instead, she said, "Well, it may have been a big misunderstanding. I mean, there I was, following you around and screaming like a lunatic. She may have thought we meant something to each other."

Jeremy laughed. "That would be pretty ridiculous, wouldn't it?"

"Maybe you should call her," Madison said, knowing he didn't know "Pinky's" phone number. "Or write her and explain."

Jeremy nodded briskly. "I'll do that."

They sat for a few moments in awkward silence. Finally, Madison clapped her hands together. "In the meantime, we have another big problem on our hands."

"You're right," Jeremy agreed. "I'm

thirsty. What do you say we go for a Coke at Ruby's favorite watering hole? My treat."

At the mention of her name, Ruby leaped to her feet, wagging her tail. Madison chuckled. "I'm up for that. And while we're at it, we can figure out what to do about Reed Rawlings."

"How do you feel about Chinese water torture?" Jeremy asked as they walked over to a sidewalk café called Poodles on the Park.

Madison grinned wickedly. "That's good for a start. And after we trash his locker, key his Beemmer, and pants him at lunch, let's hit him where he lives."

They found an outside table closest to the thick laurel hedge bordering the street, and ordered two Cokes and a bowl of water for Ruby. Then Madison outlined her plan. "Reed has proved that he'll do anything to get a hot chocolate or win an election. Two hours ago he tried to talk me into teaming up with him to beat you. I say let's beat him at his own game."

Jeremy blinked in surprise. "You mean, join forces?"

"Exactly!" Madison took a sip of her Coke. "We could run as copresidents."

Jeremy studied her face. "You'd really want to do that?"

Madison nodded firmly. "I know you and I think alike. You want to bring all of the students at Evergreen into the loop, and I want to expand the loop to include the whole town."

"Sounds like a pretty loopy plan to me," Jeremy cracked. "But I like it."

Madison held her glass in the air. "Then here's to us. Partners?"

Jeremy clinked glasses with Madison. "Partners."

15

On Saturday morning, before she'd even had breakfast or brushed her teeth, Madison made her phone calls. The first one was to Piper, who reacted true to form.

"Are you nuts?" she shrieked. "You don't need a copresident!"

"Maybe I don't," Madison replied. "But the school does. You saw how many students have joined Jeremy's marching band!"

"True," Piper admitted reluctantly. "His numbers have been rising, and it might be nice to have the two extremes at Evergreen finally get together. . . ."

"So, what's your problem?" Madison asked, switching the phone to her other ear and running a brush through her hair.

Piper hemmed and hawed for a few minutes before finally spitting it out. "I want you to swear, as my BFF," she said, "that you are doing this because you believe it's the right thing to do, *not* because you feel guilty about being an absolute witch to Jeremy for over two years."

Madison flopped back onto her bed. "I do feel guilty," she confessed. "But not so much that I'd be his copresident just to make him feel better. I believe it's the right thing." She held up her right hand, even though she knew Piper couldn't see her. "I swear."

There was a long pause. Finally Piper said, "Okay, I support you. But you do realize you're going to have to do some fast-talking to get Alex behind this idea."

Madison knew Piper was right. She also knew she had to have Alex's support to make it work. After grabbing a cup of coffee from the pot in the kitchen, she punched her old friend's number into her cell phone.

Alex listened quietly as Madison told him of Reed's incredible deception, and Jeremy's innocence, and lastly of their joint plan for winning the election. Then he asked her a surprising question. "Are you in love with Jeremy?"

Madison choked on her coffee. "Where did that come from?" she sputtered.

"Just answer my question, Maddy."

Maddy suddenly felt like she'd been hit with one of Alex's famous spotlights. "I don't know," she said, honestly. "It's only been about twelve hours since I thought he was the most evil guy on the planet. But would it matter?"

Now it was Alex's turn in the hot seat. "All right, Ms. McKay, I will admit to carrying a torch for you, especially in my youth—two months ago. And there have been moments when I've seen you look at other guys, like Jeremy, in a way that you've never looked at me, and I've felt bad. But I think I'm finally over it."

Madison didn't know how to respond. She'd always suspected that Alex cared for her in that way. Frankly, she had been relieved that he'd never dared to do anything about it.

After a long pause, Alex said, "Come on, Maddy. Aren't you going to ask the famous question—'is there someone else?'"

Madison did as she was told, dropping her voice dramatically. "Is there someone else?"

"Yes, Miss Scarlett," Alex replied in his best imitation of the old classic movie *Gone With the Wind*. "There *is* someone."

"But who can it be?" Madison replied in a terrible Southern accent.

"It's Olivia," he confessed. "I'm crazy about her!"

Madison dropped the accent. "Olivia? Who's Olivia?"

"Mouse," Alex answered impatiently. "Isn't it obvious?"

With a start, Madison realized she had been so wrapped up in her own world lately that she truly had not noticed any sparks flying between Alex and the tiny girl in the hooded sweatshirt. But she couldn't tell him that.

"You two are perfect for each other!" Maddy cried, imagining her six-foot-four-inch friend with the five-foot-tall Mouse. They certainly made an interesting pair.

"Do you really think so?" Alex asked in earnest. "Some people think I'm a little too old for her. She's just a freshman, you know."

"Alex! You are the biggest kid I know!" Madison grinned as she recalled him riding the carousel in his silly striped scarf. "No one would ever accuse you of being too old for anybody."

"Really?" Alex sounded genuinely pleased. "Thanks, Maddy."

Once they had cleared the air about their romantic interests, the two of them were really able to discuss Madison and Jeremy's co-candidacy. Alex became enthusiastically supportive, confessing that he had always liked Jeremy. He'd only shunned him out of loyalty to Madison. Alex even came up with some great ideas for their speech on Monday. "You've got the heart, and Drum's got his finger on the student pulse," he improvised. "I'd say that together, the two of you define Evergreen's Heartbeat!"

Liz Struthers was next on Madison's list. She was reluctant to call her because Liz could be so ruthless in her questions. But Liz's response was the biggest surprise of all.

"Brilliant!" Liz cried. "You and Jeremy will be the living fusion of Lincoln's best idea—creating a government *of* the people, *by* the people, and *for* the people."

"Talk about brilliant," Madison gushed. "Liz, you've just handed us the theme for our keynote speech."

By the time Liz hung up, she'd promised to call Lou, Henry, Kirk, and anyone who had ever thought of joining the "Elect Madison" committee.

Madison was psyched! When Jeremy arrived bearing bagels and lattes, she met him with the fantastic news that her friends were behind them 100 percent.

Jeremy and Madison spent the entire weekend together, working on their speech for Monday's assembly and dreaming up exciting plans for the next year.

Madison couldn't believe how much they had in common, or how much fun they had together. They filled yellow pads with ideas. They raced each other around the block to clear their brains. They visited Jeremy's grandmother and walked Ruby. On Sunday evening they practiced delivering their speech by performing it for Madison's parents and brother in her living room. Her family gave them three thumbs-up and a firm assurance that the election was in the bag.

Throughout the weekend, Madison constantly reminded Jeremy that he needed to write his "girlfriend." He kept promising he'd do it, but never seemed to get around to it.

At ten o'clock on Sunday night, Madison and Jeremy said good night. They agreed to meet before school the next day and put their plan into action.

Usually, on the night before an election, Madison was too nervous to sleep. But this night she snuggled into her bed ready to dream about her wonderful weekend. As she drifted off to sleep, she heard the *Ding!* from her computer. A new letter. Was it from Blue? Madison crawled across her bed and looked at the monitor. Yes!

She had been wondering what Jeremy would write, but this letter caught her completely by surprise.

Dear Pinky,
I'm assuming the reason I never heard back from you is because of the girl you saw me with at the Space Needle. I could tell you she doesn't mean a thing to me—but I'd be lying.

I have very strong feelings for her. I
don't know if anything will come of it,
but I just wanted to be honest with
you.

Blue

Madison was grinning from ear to ear as she
sat down at her desk to write her response.

Dear Blue,
It's true. I was there at the Space Needle. And I
promise I'll be there again. Could we just meet
once to say hello—and, if necessary, good-bye?
How about tomorrow at 4 p.m.? I'll wear the pink
rose.

Pinky

As she hit SEND, Madison slipped the
remaining rose out of her crystal vase and,
holding it like a microphone, jumped on top
of her bed. She started bouncing up and
down on the mattress and, before long, was
belting "Ain't No Mountain High Enough"
at the top of her lungs.

16

When Reed Rawlings arrived at Evergreen High the next morning, he was totally blindsided by what happened. He sat in his car, slack-jawed, staring in dismay at the sight before him. Above the front doors hung a giant banner that read: DRUM AND MCKAY FOR PRESIDENT: TWO HEARTS THAT BEAT AS ONE! Madison McKay and Jeremy Drum stood together on the front steps and greeted each student as he or she came to school.

Sierra Faith and her band of drummers had begun to play, and soon the students milling around the entrance formed an impromptu conga line. Sierra led them merrily around the school and into the auditorium, where the candidates were scheduled to make their final campaign speeches.

Once inside, the Drama Club, under the direction of Alex Kazinsky and Olivia "Mouse" Tillotson, took over. They chose the Beatles' "Come Together" as the background for their dramatic interpretation of what would happen when Jeremy and Madison joined forces.

As the music swelled over the sound system, the stage filled with fog. Dancers in white gloves, representing all the different factions of the school, moved artfully through the swirling clouds of mist under dramatic lighting effects to finally clasp hands at center stage. The effect was stunning: What looked like a chaotic whirl of humanity resolved itself into a balanced geometric form that was as beautiful as it was powerful.

When Mr. Kaufman introduced Madison and Jeremy, they emerged from the back of the stage through the fog, walking side by side. Madison and Jeremy took their places at separate podiums on opposite sides of the stage. Mouse and Alex, who were up in the grid above the auditorium, focused a pin spot on each of them. Then Madison began to speak.

"I have a story to tell, about a girl . . ."

"And a boy . . . ," Jeremy said.

"And a very big misunderstanding," they finished together.

The two of them relayed the story of that fateful Homecoming two years before, taking turns explaining what had happened, and describing how one mistake had led them to distrust and hate the other so much.

"Names were called," Madison explained. "And we each were branded."

"Never once did we speak to each other," Jeremy said.

"Never once did we allow the other to explain," Madison said.

"We accepted what others told us, and continued blindly on the path that others chose for us," Jeremy said.

"Nearly three years passed," Madison continued.

"Practically all of our high school years," Jeremy added. "Then, one day, we finally talked."

"We asked a lot of questions and listened

to the answers," Madison said, turning to face Jeremy.

"We dispensed with labels like 'preppie' or 'loser' or 'skater' or 'Goth.'" Jeremy turned to Madison.

"And we discovered that I am just a girl." Madison left her podium and walked to center stage.

"And I am just a boy." Jeremy left his podium and joined Madison.

The two clasped hands and faced the audience of students. "And together we're two different individuals with the same wish," they said. "To make a difference in this world. Two hearts that beat as one."

Madison smiled up at the students in the balcony and at the back of the auditorium. "If Jeremy and I can find a way to join hands and work together . . ."

"Then all of us can do it," Jeremy said. "What do you say, Evergreen? Is it possible?"

Several shouts of "Yes!" rang through the auditorium.

Madison put a hand to her ear. "What? I can't hear you!"

"Yes!" shouted twelve hundred voices. "Yes!"

The cheerleaders, who were in their usual spots in the front row, led the screaming, doing stag leaps and touching their toes.

Alex and Mouse circled their spotlights all over the stage, finally joining them together just as Jeremy impulsively planted a kiss on Madison's lips. The crowd went wild.

The response to the speech was thrilling, but Jeremy's kiss took Madison's breath away. The drumming began again, and for half a second Madison didn't know which was louder—Sierra's drums or her heart. Jeremy grasped her hand and, leaping off the stage, they raced up the aisle.

Reed Rawlings was supposed to give his speech next, but very few students stayed around to hear it. Most of the kids followed Jeremy and Madison out of the auditorium, clapping and dancing in the aisles as they went.

By the end of the day, after the students at Evergreen had voted, it seemed that no one even remembered Reed's name. Everyone was completely caught up in the amazing story of Madison and Jeremy.

Minutes before the final bell, Mr. Kaufman's voice came over the loudspeaker. "May I have your attention, please. The election results are in, and you students have made your choice in what I can only describe as a landslide. Ladies and gentlemen, let's hear it for next year's student council president—or, I should say, presidents—Madison McKay and Jeremy Drum!"

Raucous cheers could be heard coming out of every classroom, and echoing up and down the halls.

Piper, Alex, and Mouse met Madison as she came out of the door of Ms. Healy's American Literature class. The four of them wrapped their arms around one another and hopped in a tight circle, chanting, "We did it! We did it!"

"Wait for me!" Ultracool Liz Struthers actually ran down the hall to join the funny, hopping circle of friends that made its way through the North Hall. Lou Garcia's war whoops could be heard coming from the gym at the other end of the building. When he saw the winner's circle, which was expanding by the second, he sprinted the last ten yards like a running back heading for the goal line. He hopped over students bent down at their lockers and ducked between teachers until finally he joined the touchdown dance with the rest of the gang.

"We've got to find Jeremy," Madison cried. Her voice was getting hoarse from screaming so much. "Where's Jeremy!"

The doors to the South Hall burst open, and a new circle of jubilant teens danced into view, accompanied by frenzied drumming. Nick Torres, the skater who had nominated Jeremy, and Leonard Watkins, the computer nerd, had lifted Jeremy to their shoulders and carried him in triumph toward the main entrance. It was a lopsided carry since Leonard was so short. Luckily, Alex ran to help before Jeremy toppled over.

Lou hoisted Madison onto his shoulders and the two winning circles danced together. Madison held her hand out over the heads of her friends, and Jeremy caught hold of it. "Congratulations, partner!" he cried.

"We've got to celebrate!" Madison shouted over the noise.

"Giorgio's!" Liz's head popped up between them. "I called and reserved the whole place for our victory celebration. Four o'clock!"

"Four?" Jeremy's smile faded, but instantly returned. "I'll have to be a little late," he shouted from his perch above Liz. "I have an appointment that I can't change. But I'll be quick."

With a start, Madison remembered her rendezvous with "Blue" at the Space Needle. Suddenly she wished she hadn't arranged it for that afternoon. It sent a whole new wave of butterflies jostling around her stomach. "I'm going to be late too!" she shouted back.

She struggled to hold on to Jeremy's hand as the parade turned and marched toward Evergreen High's big front doors. Being carried by Lou, who was dancing to the beat of the drums, was like riding a bucking bronco. Then the two groups split apart, and Madison lost hold of Jeremy's hand. She watched him melt away into the surging crowd of delirious supporters.

Forty-five minutes later, Madison was finally able to break away from the party that had taken over the front lawn of the high school. She barely had enough time to run home, grab her rose, and beg her mother to drop her at the Seattle Center.

With one minute to spare, Madison arrived at the Space Needle. Her rose was hastily clipped into her short dark hair. Her cheeks were red from all of the mad rushing around. But she had made it on time.

So had Jeremy. Once again he was waiting by the elevator that rode up to the top of the Space Needle. A somewhat faded blue carnation was pinned to the lapel of his jacket.

Madison, who usually overplanned everything, hadn't taken one second to plan what she would say when she finally met "Blue" face-to-face. A man with a bouquet of balloons passed by, and she ducked out of sight behind them. As she ran alongside the vendor, she hastily tried to collect her thoughts. So much was riding on this meeting, and she didn't want to blow it.

When the balloon man got close to the elevator tower, Madison jumped out from behind the balloons and hid by a corner of the tower. Her mind was still a complete blank. But she couldn't leave Jeremy standing there for another minute. So she inched her way along the wall until she was safely hidden behind the post he was leaning against.

Madison checked the TechnoMarine watch she'd borrowed from Piper. It was nearly five minutes after four. Time was running out! She had to say *something*. But what?

Barely a foot away, she heard Jeremy exhale in frustration, and her heart sank. When he made a move to leave, her hand shot out from behind the pillar and caught hold of his.

"Blue?" she whispered. "Please don't turn around."

Jeremy didn't move. "Okay," he said warily.

"I'm trying to find the words to tell you what our letters have meant to me," she whispered. "And how much your friendship means to me."

Jeremy nodded. "It's been important to me, too." He started to turn around, but Madison tugged his arm, hard.

"Don't look, yet. Please!"

Jeremy quickly turned his head away. "All right, but—"

Madison didn't let him finish. She squeezed her eyes shut and started babbling. "I didn't know who you were until last Friday—which, incidentally, turned out to be about the most important day of my life. And when I knew it was you, I just didn't know how to tell you that I was me. You once told me I was cold and heartless, and I just couldn't bear it if you said it again. Everything has been so perfect, I just don't want to blow it, and now that we're standing here holding hands, I don't want to let go—"

"So don't," a voice whispered, very close to her cheek.

Madison's eyes popped open, and she found herself staring into Jeremy's sparkling baby blues. And for a moment, time seemed to stop. She noticed that Jeremy had very long eyelashes for a boy. She saw that there was a tiny freckle above his perfectly shaped lips. And he smelled delicious—like spicy soap. Slowly, she raised her hand and touched the lock of dark hair that fell forward over his forehead. It was as soft as she imagined it would be.

She tilted her face up to meet his, so

close that their lips were almost touching, and asked, "You haven't said anything. Are you mad?"

"I always have been," Jeremy murmured. "Mad about you . . ."

Ever so slowly the distance between their lips disappeared. In that one tingling moment the past, with every painful memory of humiliation, melted completely away.

Jeremy slipped his arm around Madison's waist and pressed her close against him. She wrapped her arms around his neck. They were a perfect fit, just as she had dreamed they would be.

Pinky and Blue—two hearts beating as one.

Make sure to catch the next Love Letters book:
💜 *Mixed Messages* 💜

"That's it!" Jade yelled. "He lives on Sycamore. Turn!"

"I know this street," Adam said as he turned right onto a street bordered by mature sycamore trees and older homes. "What's the address?"

"I-I don't remember," Jade confessed. "But it's got a little studio in back."

The fourth house on the left had a cottage in back and Jade tapped Adam on the shoulder. "Stop here. This could be it." "Couldn't be," Adam said, without slowing down. "That's Zephyr Strauss's house."

"Stop!" Jade shrieked. "That's who I'm going to see."

Adam slowed down and pulled into an empty driveway. He stopped the car, then turned to look at Jade. "Why didn't you say so? I know Zephyr. I didn't know he belonged to a study group."

"It—it's not a study group, exactly," she stammered. Jade could feel the red crawl up her neck to her face as she realized she'd been caught in her lie. "I just said study group because, well, it was kind of complicated to explain to Miss Perkins and the others. Actually, we *are* studying music. Zephyr asked me to jam with the group today."

Jade could see by his expression that Adam knew Zephyr meant more to her than she'd let on.

"I understand," he said finally. Adam turned the car around and they rode back to Zephyr's house in silence. Jade felt terrible. She'd told a lie and now everything felt awkward. "Adam, thank you for a wonderful picnic," Jade said, as she got out of the van. She grabbed her guitar from the back and ran around to his side of the van. "I mean it. I love your family, and your whole weird, wacky life." A smile crept slowly across Adam's face. Then he touched the tip of her nose with his fingertip. "I've been waiting for the longest time," he murmured. "And suddenly—here you are."

Jade stood on the curb and watched Adam drive away. His words were simple and sweet, and she longed to hear more.